John Peel is the author of numerous best-selling novels for young adults, including installments in the *Star Trek, Are You Afraid of the Dark?* and *Where in the World Is Carmen Sandiego?* series. He is also the author of many acclaimed novels of science fiction, horror, and suspense.

Mr. Peel currently lives on the outer rim of the Diadem, on a planet popularly known as Earth.

BOOK OF OCEANS

John Peel

Llewellyn Publications
Woodbury, Minnesota

First Llewellyn Edition
First printing, 2005

Cover design by Gavin Dayton Duffy
Cover illustration © 2005 by Bleu Turrell / Artworks
Project management and editing by Rhiannon Ross

Llewellyn is a registered trademark of Llewellyn Worldwide, Ltd.

Library of Congress Cataloging-in-Publication Data
Peel, John, 1954–
Book of Oceans / by John Peel.
    p. cm. -- (Diadem, Worlds of Magic; #8)
Summary: When Oracle suggests a comforting vacation through a portal to a world of water, he fails to mention that it is also a world inhabited by pirates.
ISBN 0-7387-0748-1
[1. Magic--Fiction. 2. Fantasy.] I.Title.
PZ7.P348Boo2005

Llewellyn Publications
A Division of Llewellyn Worldwide, Ltd.
2143 Wooddale Drive, Dept. 0-7387-0748-1
Woodbury, MN 55125-2989, U.S.A.
www.llewellyn.com

Printed in the United States of America

This is for Rozlynn Wander

PROLOGUE

The Harvesters were working hard. The men were using their long-handled scythes to cut the sea wheat, and the women used the scoops to gather the falling grain before it fell back into the sea, to be lost forever. The gentle rocking of their boats didn't disturb the rhythm of their long-practiced movement. The sun was high in the sky, but it wasn't time yet for the noon break.

Lahra didn't pause in her actions, but her eyes skimmed the horizon. Harvesting was *good*, and it was necessary, but it was also so infernally *dull*. She didn't know how the others managed to keep their minds on their task, but it was hard for her. She didn't want to be catching and storing grain from the floating fields, far out on the seas—she wanted to be off in her small boat, exploring. She had dreams that one day she would discover one of the rare islands, and walk upon land that didn't undulate under your feet with the rise and ebb of the waters.

But, she knew it was a foolish dream. Her parents, and their parents, and *their* parents had all been Harvesters, and a Harvester was all she would ever be, either. It was her lot in life to gather the grain, and, in the evenings around the pots of fire, to winnow and grind the grain, and then to bake bread. Some day, she would marry a Harvester, and would raise children, and they, in their turn, would also become Harvesters.

It was all so horribly *dull*! She longed for excitement, some kind of adventure—anything! But, of course, it never changed from day to day. She'd been born to float the seas, and when she eventually died, her old, withered body would be slipped beneath the surface, and she'd sink down into the dark depths, where the scavenger fish would eat their fill of her. What a prospect to look forward to!

Oops! She almost missed her scoop. Correcting quickly, she caught the falling stalks and brought them to her boat, depositing them in the barrels with practiced skill. Then out with the scoop again, ready for the next catch.

Her eyes narrowed slightly as she saw a flash of color out to sea, beyond the floating wheat island. What could it be? Perhaps a messenger from her village? No, that was floating to the east, and this sail was coming from the north. Lahra felt a sudden surge of excitement. Perhaps these were visitors from some other village, a village the restless ocean currents may have carried near theirs! They would be *strangers*, someone new to talk with. She grinned to herself. Maybe even flirt with, a little. Someone new!

She wasn't the only one who'd noticed the sail, of course. "Visitors," old Calen said, gruffly. He always sounded like he was unhappy. Nobody could recall ever having seen him smile. "Wonder what they want?"

"Not you, I'll wager," Munson answered, laughing. "Maybe it's traders? It's been a while since any have been around."

3

That was an interesting thought! Traders, with a store of wonders to look through! Lahra wasn't the only one who found the thought exciting. Everyone started discussing the possibilities that the sail meant—though the work didn't slow down, of course. The harvesting must be accomplished. Everyone had an opinion, thought, or comment, and the conversation almost soared for once. Lahra didn't see much point in trying to guess what the strangers wanted—all they had to do was to wait for the ship to arrive, and then they'd find out. She listened to the happy, idle chatter, but didn't speak herself. Instead, she focused whatever attention she had left from her work on watching the sail grow larger.

It wasn't a single sail, she soon discovered, but a number of them, all on the same ship. She was amazed—to carry so many sails, the ship had to be enormous! She'd never seen anything larger than a twelve-person catamaran in her life, and that needed only one sail. This ship must be a monster! And so it proved, as it drew closer. She could make out that it had three tall masts, and one jutting forward from the prow. All held several sails, and she could see that people were running about on ropes around the sails. They were being furled, and the ship was losing some of its speed. Whoever was on the ship aimed to stop and talk, it seemed. And the ship was immense! It had to be more than a hundred feet in length, and twenty or more wide. Why, a ship that large could carry . . . Well, at least dozens of people, and maybe even more than a hundred. It was like a whole village itself!

It was drawing closer and slowing further. She could see it rising and falling with the power of the waves it sliced through, and the people aboard it were moving from the sails down to the decks. Many were gathering at the sides of the vessel, obviously ready to call greetings. Were they as excited as Lahra and her friends? They seemed to be moving around a lot, and waving.

Finally, the ship was virtually upon them, and Lahra couldn't help admiring it. Up close, it was even more astonishing. Where had they ever found enough wood to build something that enormous? Lahra had never seen a tree taller than six feet, but the planks that this great ship was made from had to be more than twenty feet long! How could such trees ever be grown in a floating village?

Spume kicked up by the vessel sprayed across her skin, tingling in the sun. It felt wonderful, and she wanted to stop working to call a greeting. But that was

Munson's responsibility, not hers. She'd just wait, and listen. She'd have her chance to chatter later. Naturally, curious as they were, none of the villagers had stopped harvesting.

"Stand down!" a voice came from the deck of the ship, more than twenty feet above their heads. "Put down those implements, and stand ready to come aboard."

Lahra was puzzled; didn't these people know that Harvesters had their work to do, and couldn't stop merely to talk? Well, even if they didn't, Munson did. Without a pause in his scything, he called back: "A greeting to you all."

"The blazes with greetings!" the voice snarled back. "Do as you're told!"

Munson looked as puzzled as Lahra felt. "But we're Harvesters," he protested. "We have our work to do!"

"You have *new* work to do," the man yelled down. "Put down those tools, and come aboard." For the first time, Lahra saw that there were woven ladders hanging over the side of the ship, and men at the top, gesturing for the Harvesters to climb them.

"I'm sorry, friend," Munson answered. "But we have our work to do."

"Stupid peasants," growled the man, and now Lahra was alarmed. There was a sharp snapping sound, and something whistled through the air. Munson gave a loud cry, and spun about before falling into the bottom of their small boat. Lahra stared at him in shock. There was an arrow sticking out of his shoulder, and blood was pouring from the wound.

"They're *attacking* us!" she gasped, too stunned to even go to Munson's aid. The rest of the Harvesters were just as stunned; they had all stopped working.

"And the rest of you will get worse if we have to come down there after you!" the man on the ship threatened. "Now—put down those tools, and start climbing! Two of you bring that fool with you."

Lahra slowly did as she'd been commanded. More of the men at the side of the ship above them had bows ready to fire, and she knew that they would, indeed, use them as they threatened. The rest of the Harvesters seemed to understand this, too. Their scythes and scoops tumbled into the bottom of their boats, and with shocked faces they all started to climb the rope ladders.

Rough hands grabbed Lahra's wrists as she reached the top, and two savage-looking men dragged her onto the deck, clearly not caring that they were bruising her. "What's going on?" she asked them. "Why are you doing this?"

The taller, uglier of the two men slapped her across the face. "Quiet!" he snarled. "Slaves speak only when asked a direct question!"

Slaves? Lahra looked about her on the ship. The men—and they were all men—were armed with daggers and swords as well as bows. Lahra's people used such weapons only to hunt fish, not *people*. What was wrong with these men?

One of them stepped forward, a wide grin on his evil-looking face. "Welcome to your new lives," he greeted them. "Welcome to Hell."

1

"I can't take it any more!" Score yelled, throwing his hands up in disgust. "Those two girls are driving me crazy!" He was pacing up and down the room, too agitated to sit down.

Pixel seemed to be quite calm, though, stretched out on his bed. He'd been relaxing after practicing some new spells from "The Book of Magic." Spell casting was quite tiring, as Score knew from his own experience. "So, why don't you tell them?" he suggested.

Score glared at him. "I *have* told them. Over and over again. Nothing seems to get through their thick skulls. Helaine just scowls and tells me to mind my own business or she'll chop off my arm and beat me unconscious with it. I *think* that's her idea of a joke, but I'm not taking any chances. She can be kind of literal, you know. And as for Jenna . . ."

Pixel sat up, and frowned. "And what's wrong with Jenna?" he demanded.

This was a touchy subject, because Score knew that Pixel was very fond of the girl. "She's even worse," Score complained. "She just turns those big, deer-like eyes on me, and I haven't the heart to yell at her."

"She's very sensitive," Pixel said, smiling slightly.

"Not where Helaine's concerned." Score shook his head. "You'd think that after six months, the two girls would have at least learned how to be civil to one another. But, no—they're worse than ever."

"It's hard for them to get along," Pixel pointed out. "Their people have such a long history of hating one another . . ."

"I know." Score sighed; he *did* know, and he did understand. Prejudice was very hard to overcome. The two girls were both from the same area of the same planet, but they couldn't possibly be less alike. Helaine had been raised the somewhat spoiled daughter of one of the most powerful nobles on the planet. As if that hadn't been enough, she'd also disguised herself as a boy and taken lessons in fighting. She'd proven to be better at it than the real boys—until her secret had been uncovered. As a result, she tended to be very willful, and often aggressive. She tended to chop things up with her sword first, and then stop and think about them afterward—if at all. Initially, Score had been furious when he discovered that "Renald" was actually a girl, and a better fighter than he was, but he'd learned to calm down and just accept it. Now he felt very differently about Helaine . . .

Enough of that! He wasn't even going to remember that her father had wanted Score to marry Helaine. Hey, they were good friends now, and he wasn't going to mess things up by getting romantically involved with her. No way!

So, Jenna—Jenna was a peasant, low-born and raised in pretty near grinding poverty. Peasants worked for the lords on Ordin, and were supposed to consider themselves to be lucky to be allowed even that. In fact, most of the peasants hated the lords for taxing them and keeping them in fear for their lives. Jenna hated more than most, because she'd been a hedge witch, a healer, and she'd been forced to deal with the poor folks injuries, trying to make a living. Peasants were often caught between two armies of professional soldiers when the lords had a squabble. Whatever happened, the peasants suffered. As a result, Jenna was very sympathetic and very sweet to everyone—except the nobles.

And now, here they were—the two girls who loathed one another, trying to live in the same castle on the world of Dondar, and not kill one another. It wasn't working out, no matter what they tried. Pixel could usually get people to do as he wished, but even he'd given up in disgust with the girls. Score wasn't the most patient person in the world—or *any* world—and he was almost ready to scream.

He and Pixel had rather naively thought, six months ago when Jenna had agreed to join them, that the girls would get used to one another, maybe even like each other, and it would all blow over. Instead, it seemed like the situation was getting worse every day. If Helaine wanted a bath, then you could be certain Jenna had just decided to take one and used all of the hot water. If Jenna wanted to play in the courtyard with her unicorn friend Smoke, then Helaine and *her* friend Flame were already there.

Even the unicorns—who were best friends—couldn't get their humans to cooperate. And it was almost impossible to refuse a unicorn anything.

"So," Score finally growled, "what are we going to do about the situation?"

"I was hoping we could ignore it till it went away," Pixel confessed.

"Coward!"

"Where the girls are concerned, yes," Pixel agreed. "I like them both, and I don't want either of them mad at me."

"I like them both—individually," Score stated. "It's just when they're on the same planet that there's trouble."

"What do you want to do?" Pixel asked angrily. "Send Jenna back home?" He crossed his arms. "I won't agree to that."

"I know you won't," Score snapped. "You're too lovey-dovey with her for that."

"And what's wrong with that?" Pixel demanded. "She's a lovely girl, and I'm very fond of her."

"There's nothing wrong with being fond of her— except it clouds your judgment," Score pointed out.

"Oh, really?" Pixel jumped to his feet and waved his index finger in Score's face. "And what about you and Helaine, then?"

Score felt his face going red. "What about me and Helaine?" he demanded. "We're not the ones going around the castle holding hands and giving each other sickly smiles."

"Oh, and that's supposed to convince me you two aren't an item?"

"We're *not* an item!" Score protested. "Well, except in her demented father's mind, and I don't think either of us want to make him happy."

"Face reality, Score," Pixel jeered. "You're stuck on her."

"My fist will be stuck on your nose in a minute," Score growled, shaking it in Pixel's face. "I've got better things to do with my time than get into a romantic relationship with Helaine, okay?"

"Come at a bad time, have I?" a fresh voice asked.

Score whirled around to see their odd friend Oracle looking at them, his arms crossed, a smile on his long face. As ever, he was dressed in black, and looking vaguely transparent. Score had never been able to figure out exactly what Oracle was, and Oracle hated explaining mysteries, so he refused to talk. He could pop in and out of any world, it seemed, at will. He also had a very bad habit of being the bearer of bad news.

"If you're here, then the bad times are sure to follow," Score growled. "What's the problem now?"

"No problem," Oracle replied, walking through the bed to join them. "It's just that I haven't seen you all for a while, and thought I'd drop in to see how you're doing. Not too well, it would appear."

"It's the girls," Score and Pixel both complained at the same time.

Oracle raised an eyebrow. "Well, at least you're in agreement as to what the problem is. I wonder if they'd agree?"

"They wouldn't even agree on whether the sun had come up," Score muttered. "If one said it had, the other would argue it was still night."

"Ah!" Oracle smiled again. "Female problems, I take it?"

"You can say that again," Pixel agreed. "I think we need expert advice. I mean, we're only teenagers, and . . ." He blushed. "I really don't know that much about girls."

"Really?" Score snapped. "I thought you were an expert on everything."

"Don't start on me, Score," Pixel growled.

"Guys, guys!" Oracle held up his hands. "Don't let *their* problems get you at each other's throats."

"You're right," Score said, shaking his head. "It's just that I'm so tense from their fighting that I yell at Pix because he's safer."

Pixel nodded. "Yes, same here. Listen, Oracle, what do you know about girls?"

Oracle laughed. "Even less than you do, I fear. I may *look* human, but I'm not. And there are no females of my species around for me to learn anything about. No, you need to talk to a *real* expert."

Score and Pixel looked at one another, puzzled, and then Pixel grinned. "Shanara!"

"Oh yeah," Score agreed. "She's *definitely* female. I think . . ."

Shanara was a magician who was a friend of theirs. Though her magic was not as strong as theirs, she was older than they were, and far more skilled. Her specialty was the magic of illusions, at which she was a genius. She could make herself—or other people— look like anything she wished. In fact, each time they saw her, she tended to look a little different—mostly in her hair color and style, which she enjoyed changing. The problem was—she *looked* like a pin-up girl, but Score couldn't be certain that this was what she actually was. For all he knew, she might be a hundred years old and a wrinkled crone. Or a child. With the strength of her illusions, there was simply no way of knowing.

"You think she'll help us?" Score asked. Not only was he keen on resolving the Helaine/Jenna problem, but he enjoyed seeing Shanara.

"We can ask," Oracle said, spreading his hands. He closed his eyes and concentrated a moment. A few seconds later, there was a swirling mist in the air that solidified into what Shanara chose to look like today. It was all an illusion, of course—she was still in her own castle on her own world—but it was certainly a spectacular one.

She was tall, and very athletic, wearing a long, flowing blue robe. Her hair today was also long and flowing, but a pure, sparkling silver color. Her blue eyes danced with humor as they flickered from person to person.

"So," she said, "I understand you're having girl trouble. Welcome to the adult world."

"We're not having any problems," Score protested. "It's the girls who have the problems."

"They hate one another," Pixel added.

"Ah." Shanara paced up and down the room. Since she was an illusion, she tended to walk through objects like the bed, table, and chairs. "And this is causing you some grief?"

"We just want them to get along," Pixel said. "It's horrible living in the same castle with them while they're fighting."

"And they're *always* fighting," Score added.

"I see." Shanara knew their story, and she knew why the girls hated one another. She chewed on her lower lip for a moment before speaking again. "Maybe you need a break?"

"What do you mean?" Oracle asked, interested.

"Well, the four of you have been cooped up in this castle together for several months now," Shanara explained. "You haven't been off saving the Diadem, or even just exploring. I'm sure Jenna and Helaine *want* to get along, but sometimes it's hard to do that when you're breathing down each other's necks all the time.

And when you're thrown together constantly, small irritations become large sores."

Score grinned. "Shanara, you're brilliant!" he exclaimed. "That's it, exactly. Two girls, cooped together, who can't stand one another, forced to see each other all the time, knowing that the other will be around the next corner—"

"We get the picture," Pixel said. "They get on one another's nerves." He rubbed his blue chin thoughtfully. "Maybe a rest would be a good idea at that. But where?"

Score laughed. "You know what I always wanted to do? Go on a cruise."

"A cruise?" Pixel sounded confused. Score tended to forget that Pixel's world didn't share everything with Earth.

"It's a big boat," Score explained. "It goes somewhere fun, with lots of sun and sand and water. You just laze around, eat food all day, and do nothing as long as you like."

Pixel frowned. "It sounds . . . unproductive."

"That's the idea, you workaholic you!" Score laughed. "And the girls all wear bikinis . . . Mmmmm!"

"What's bikinis?"

19

There was no stopping Score now, though. "I wonder if there's anything like that in the Diadem? I don't think the Disney Cruise Line will take payment in precious jewels. And they like passports and other such nonsense that we don't have."

"What are passports?"

Oracle stepped in smoothly. "I know of a world that *might* fit your requirements," he said. "It's called Brine. About ninety percent of the surface is water. The people there are mostly peaceful, and they are, of course, the most skilled sailors."

"Sounds perfect!" Score enthused. "Tropical beaches, sultry maidens in practically nothing, lots of sun and sand . . . Come on, let's break the good news to the girls!" He rushed off. Pixel threw up his hands and followed.

Shanara's image turned to that of Oracle. "What are you up to?" she asked him, suspiciously.

"Me?" Oracle tried to look the picture of innocence, and failed miserably. "I'm just trying to give them what they need."

"They *need* a vacation," Shanara said, firmly.

"Nonsense," Oracle replied. "That's their problem—they've sat around for too long, doing practically nothing. What they *need* is to get their blood going again."

"And you *do* intend to mention the pirates?" Shanara asked.

"I think we should let them discover that part for themselves," Oracle suggested. "They're not babies—we don't have to hold their hands for them."

"I see." Shanara glared at him. "So you want them to get their blood going again? It sounds to me like it will be *flowing* again . . ."

2

Helaine was attempting to keep her temper in check. She knew how explosive she could be at times, and how the others disliked her when she blew up. But it wasn't fair to blame her *all* of the time! It was mostly because she was horribly provoked by that wretch, Jenna.

She had tried—she *really* had. Score—curse the sadistic fiend!—had made her promise to try and let the past go, and make friends with Jenna. So

22

Helaine had, however reluctantly, gone along with his request. But Jenna, it seemed, was not making any effort of her own to get along. Pixel was impossible, of course—he was completely enchanted by Jenna, so he could never see that she might do anything wrong. Helaine knew this, and gave him extra leeway because of it. Pixel's problem was that he was still not used to dealing with *real* people. He'd been brought up living in virtual reality, and never knowing whether the "people" he met were real or artificial.

Helaine couldn't really understand this concept. People were either real, or they were not. She imagined it had to be something like Shanara's ability to create realistic illusions, though Pixel swore that there was no magic involved. Anyway, once Pixel had emerged from this web of deceit and entered the real world, he was almost as helpless as a baby. He'd had a crush on Helaine for a while. Pixel didn't know that Helaine had ever noticed this, as she'd pretended to be completely oblivious. She *liked* Pixel a whole lot, but not in that way. She was glad, in one sense, that he'd found Jenna to transfer this crush onto. Jenna was much more the sort of person who Pixel needed, she had to admit, even to herself. Pixel was gentle, thoughtful, and incredibly intelligent. What he didn't know was that he made Helaine feel almost stupid. His world was hundreds of years more advanced than hers, and she was like a baby compared to him. They could never have been equals.

Of course, Jenna could never be his equal, either—but that wasn't important to Jenna. Jenna was a *peasant*, someone almost beneath Helaine's heel, far below her in station. *She* didn't need to feel like anyone's equal—she was used to being a nothing, so she might as well be Pixel's plaything as anyone else's. A status that was beneath Helaine's dignity was certainly not beneath Jenna's! And Pixel was such a sweet person that, even though Jenna was so unworthy, he'd treat her well. It was a splendid compromise, the sort her father would be proud of.

If only Jenna could remember her place! She was *nothing*, and had to recall that when she was around Helaine. But the brat simply wouldn't! She kept trying to pretend that she was as good as Helaine, when this clearly wasn't the case. Why couldn't Score, at least, see this? *He* wasn't in love with the little wretch—at least, Helaine was pretty sure he wasn't. Score *did* tend to have an eye for a pretty girl—and for a peasant,

Jenna *was* quite fetching. If you liked the doe-eyed, subservient, stupid type. Some boys did, she knew.

Did Score?

Then she was annoyed with herself. What difference did it make what kind of girl Score liked? It wasn't like she and he were engaged, or even—what was that term Score used? Oh, yes, *dating*. Oh, sure, her father had *tried* to get them engaged, once it turned out that Score was actually the long-lost heir to the throne of Ordin— what a match *that* would have been for the house of Votrin! Then she blushed. She'd almost forgotten that the reason she'd left Ordin in the first place was to escape an arranged marriage. She wouldn't let her father get into her private life like that again—not now that she was out from under his control. She didn't want to marry *anyone*! And she knew that Score wasn't interested. He liked being free. That was why he had avoided taking up the throne of Ordin, and had fled the planet as fast as possible. He even refused to talk about it, and Helaine was forced to drop the subject.

But if anyone were to be on her side, it ought to be Score! And he was treating her like this was all *her* fault, just because Jenna was impossible to get along with!

Helaine wanted to hack something to death with her sword. She'd feel *much* better afterward . . . preferably that obnoxious brat, Jenna. But if she did that, the boys were annoying enough that they'd never speak to her again. Besides, she'd get peasant blood all over the blade of her sword, and contaminate it forever.

Plus, if she was honest with herself, she might want Jenna gone, but she didn't particularly want her dead. And she certainly didn't really want to kill anyone. She grinned to herself. Maybe just maim her a bit . . .

She was shaken out of contemplating the sorts of injuries she could deal Jenna when the object of her disgust walked into the dining room. Jenna immediately tensed, as did Helaine. She wouldn't be civil, Helaine knew, so there was no point even attempting it herself.

"I didn't know you were here," Jenna said, stiffly.

"I was just leaving," Helaine said, equally annoyed. "You're welcome to stay." There, *that* was polite—anyone could see that she was trying to be kind to the little creep.

"I see." Helaine could sense the anger and disgust in the other girl's voice. Her temper started to rise.

"What do you mean by that?" she demanded.

"What do I mean by *what*?" Jenna asked, angrily.

"Don't take that tone of voice with your betters," Helaine growled.

"*Better?*" Jenna snapped. "You'd be hard pressed to find a skunk that you're better than!"

Before Helaine could scream a reply, Score and Pixel dashed into the room, interrupting her train of thought.

"Oh, good," Score said, as oblivious to her feelings as ever. "You're together. Great. We have some exciting news. You tell 'em, Pix."

"We're going on a vacation," Pixel said, looking very happy. Helaine had absolutely no idea why. Neither, it was clear, did Jenna.

"What's a vacation?" they both asked, together.

"Ah," Score said, trying to sound smart. "Medieval world problem again. You guys don't have vacations there, do you?"

"If I knew what one was," Helaine pointed out with all of the calm she could muster, "I might be able to answer that."

"Good point," Score agreed, cheerfully. "It's when you kick back and do nothing all day long."

"I see," Helaine said, frostily. "Like your everyday life?"

"Oooh, somebody got off the rack on the wrong side this morning," Score replied. "Nice insult, though."

Pixel shook his head. "Perhaps I'd better explain?" he asked. "The idea is that you take time off from your everyday life, go somewhere different, and just enjoy yourself doing only restful or fun things. No work, no responsibilities, just fun."

Jenna perked up. "That sounds . . . interesting," she admitted. "Of course, on Ordin, we peasants never had the time to relax—we were forced to work all of our lives to pay taxes to the stinking nobles."

Trust her to start up trouble again! "And we nobles had to learn to fight, and to keep order, so you peasants could live your lives," Helaine snapped back. "I certainly never had the time to sit back and relax."

"Fine, then you're both *way* overdue," Pixel said, clearly trying to halt the growing argument. "Score had an idea for what we could do."

"Good," Jenna said, in that mock-sweet voice of hers. "I'm sure it's very clever."

"I'm sure it's very clever," Helaine repeated, mocking her. "Don't try sucking up to Score! I'm sure he can see through your wiles, even if Pixel can't."

"I'm not trying anything of the sort!" Jenna yelled. "I just think Score is very smart, that's all."

"She only thinks that because she doesn't know me well enough yet," Score said hastily, stepping in between the two girls. "She'll soon learn the truth."

"It seems to me," Shanara said from the doorway, "that the boys are right—you *do* all need a break from this place." Helaine was pleased to see Shanara, who was always very intelligent. The magician strode across the room to join them. "I've been quite intrigued by Score's stories of his home planet, Dirt—"

"Earth," Score corrected her.

"Earth," Shanara continued. "So I've been studying it. I think I can create illusions to show you what he's talking about as he explains his idea for a vacation."

"Great—a multi-media presentation!" Score enthused. "Right, I thought we needed something like a cruise. I've heard a lot about them, but I've never been on one. First slide!"

Shanara seemed to have as little idea what this meant as Helaine, but she gestured and brought up an image, floating in the air. It was of a boat of some kind, though it didn't have any masts or sails, so Helaine couldn't understand what made it move.

"It's on fire!" Jenna exclaimed, pointing at smoke rising from several tall, thick cylinders.

"That's from the engines," Score said. "It's supposed to be like that. Can we go to a close-up?" he asked Shanara. "This is really neat!"

It was as if they were flying down toward the boat. It grew and grew, and Helaine was amazed at how large it seemed to be. Then she saw that there were people on the decks, and realized it was *immense*. "I've never seen a boat that large in my life," she confessed.

"I've never seen the *sea* before," Jenna added.

"You haven't?" Pixel asked, surprised. "Oh, of course you wouldn't have. You hardly ever left your village. Trust me, you'll love it. It's so restful."

"You're one to talk," Score scoffed. "You've probably never seen a *real* sea in your life. I used to almost live on one, back in New York. But you're right, it's restful. Especially on a beach, with a cold glass of soda and a bunch of girls in bikinis . . ."

"What are bikinis?" Jenna asked.

Helaine had a bad feeling about this. The one time she'd gone to Earth, Score had expected her to wear clothing that revealed far too much of her skin in public. The females of Earth seemed to enjoy seeing how immoral they could be.

"Bikinis" turned out to be a lot worse than she could have even imagined. Shanara conjured up a picture of several girls on a beach hitting a big ball of some sort. The females only wore *very* short strips of clothing that covered almost nothing. Helaine wasn't surprised to see that Jenna was as shocked as she was.

"There is *no* way I would ever be so exposed!" she exclaimed. "That is disgusting!" She glared at Pixel. "You shouldn't even be looking at an illusion of such . . . shameless girls!" He *had* obviously been enjoying the view, but now he blushed and tried to look innocent.

Helaine glared at Score. "The girls of your world must be horrible people," she growled. "The only person I would ever allow to see so much of my skin is my husband!"

"With an attitude like that, you'll never get one," Score shot back. He rolled his eyes. "Jeez, Pix, did we get the most inhibited girlfriends ever!"

"I am *not* inhibited," Helaine snapped. "I simply have moral standards. And I'm *not* your girlfriend—as you so frequently point out!"

"She is correct," Jenna said, frostily. "It is obscene to wear so little—and in public, too."

"It figures," Score said, sighing. "The only time these two ever agree on anything, and it has to be that we're a couple of creeps." He turned to Shanara. "Hey, you're a woman of the world—worlds, in fact. Do *you* think it's obscene to wear a bikini?"

Shanara laughed, gently. "There are worlds where it is considered obscene to wear any form of clothing whatsoever. They consider covering up what God had given you as a blasphemy."

"I'd like to go there," Score said. Then he saw the filthy look that Helaine threw him, and backtracked, quickly. "Purely for research, of course!"

"Of course." Helaine could hear the amused mockery in Shanara's voice. "But," the magician continued, "Helaine and Jenna are from a world with very different values. One of the reasons they are constantly arguing is because it is hard for them to forget their values. You must respect their beliefs, and not attempt to make them change too quickly."

"Of course," Pixel agreed.

"But they won't get a good tan if they refuse to expose any skin," Score objected.

"What's a tan?" the girls asked, together.

"This is hopeless," Score decided. "Maybe we should try a safari instead."

"What's a—" the girls began, and then stopped as he glared at them.

Oracle had been listening in with some amusement. "I think your first thought was good," he commented. "And Brine would be the perfect place for you all. All you need is to open a Portal to it, and try it out. I'm sure the girls will get the idea pretty quickly."

Score brightened up. "Yeah, even these prudes can't sit on a beach in all *that* clothing and be comfortable." He grinned at Helaine. "I'll bet you've got really great legs under all that armor."

"You," she promised him, annoyed, "are not likely to find out."

"You'll bake if you wear metal," he warned her.

"Then I shall wear a dress," she vowed, even though she didn't really like them. But her dresses were all floor length, and would stop him from getting unhealthy ideas about her legs.

"This isn't shaping up to be much fun," he complained.

"Your idea of fun and mine are quite different, it seems," Helaine replied. "Perhaps I should bring along a couple of swords and teach you how to fight, at last? If you like the sight of bare flesh, you'll *love* looking at all the bruises you'll get."

"Thanks, but I do like to avoid pain," he said. "Especially involving me. Why don't you go change, and then we can set about making a Portal. Jenna's getting very good at them."

That annoyed Helaine again; was Score rubbing it in that *she* wasn't really that good at it yet? It infuriated her that the peasant should be able to outdo her there. "Maybe you'd prefer to hang out with her, then?" Helaine suggested, angrily. "After all, she's a peasant, with low standards. *She* might even let you look at her ankles."

"Be still my beating heart," Score said, mockingly. "She's Pix's girl."

"And that doesn't make me yours," Helaine retorted.

"Absolutely not!" Score agreed, throwing up his hands in surrender. "You're your own girl, I know that. I hope you enjoy the company you'll be keeping, in that case." He wandered off. Helaine glanced around. Pixel and Jenna had already left, presumably to change into traveling clothes. She was alone with the two illusions.

"Are you both absolutely sure this is a good idea?" she asked them.

"Completely," Oracle answered, with one of his grins. "This time together is *precisely* what you need."

Helaine looked to Shanara, who seemed somehow reluctant to answer. Then the magician sighed. "I hope it is the right thing," she said. "Helaine, I know that you and Jenna are having problems. Part of it must be because she intruded on you when you were the only girl with the boys."

"I'm not *jealous* of her!" Helaine protested. "And I don't mind sharing. Only . . ."

"Only not with *her*," Shanara finished. "I do understand, believe me. One day, I shall have to tell you my own story. Not now, though. But I do understand what you are going through. All I can say is that you will be a better person once you work out this trouble with Jenna. And *she* will be better for it also. So, yes, I think this trip is a good idea, in the long run."

"And in the short run?" Helaine asked.

"It's likely to be a terrible strain on you," Shanara admitted.

"Wonderful." Helaine sighed. "I can see that this idea of a *vacation* is not one I shall ever learn to like."

3

Pixel stepped through the Portal onto Brine with a curious mixture of feelings. He was excited about taking a vacation, and happy to be with Jenna anywhere; but he was also a little worried. He'd never been a very good swimmer, since that was one thing you couldn't really practice in virtual reality, and Oracle had said that so much of this world was covered with oceans. They weren't even stepping onto dry land, exactly.

Jenna's Portal had done its job well, getting them not only to Brine but also to what was the next best thing to solid land on this world—one of the floating islands. Pixel looked around in fascination as the Portal closed behind the four of them. "Cool," he muttered. The tang of salt and the soft spray of water from the sea was quite refreshing.

The "island" was actually made from interlinked plants that grew on the surface of Brine's oceans. They were thick and tough with large, flat leaves and stems that were more than two feet thick. This island was almost half a mile across, its base the tightly-linked stems. He could feel the ebb and swell of the waves beneath his feet, and it made him a little queasy not to have firm land underneath him. It also made the world look a little odd, as ripples of movement passed through the plants with the passing of the waves.

There were several houses built on the island, all made from the cut and shaped stems of a similar plant. The homes looked rather like old log cabins, burned dark in the sunlight. There were people here, too, of course, all at their work, though many had looked up when the Portal had appeared and the travelers had stepped through.

One woman came hurrying over, drying her hands on her apron, a big smile on her face. Pixel had been worried that the natives might have a fear of magic, as so many humans seemed to have on the Diadem worlds, but was relieved to discover that this was not the case for once. "Hello!" the woman called cheerfully. "We don't get many visitors here."

"You might get more if your floor stayed in one place," Score muttered.

"Ignore him," Pixel said. "We're very glad to be here."

"And we're glad you've come to visit," the woman replied. "Will you be staying long?"

"Only till I throw up," Score complained.

"This was your idea," Helaine reminded him, smirking slightly. She seemed to be completely unaffected by the rise and fall of the plants.

"Then I promise not to blame you for it," Score said.

The woman stared at Score curiously. "What is wrong with him?"

"I think he's a bit seasick," Pixel explained.

"Seasick?" The woman shook her head. "How can the sea make him ill? Has he not lived on it all of his life, like the rest of us?"

"No," Pixel replied. "We're not from your world—we come from one where we live on dry land."

"How sad for you," the woman answered. "No wonder, then, that you've come here, you poor things. You must have realized how much better life is here on Brine."

"We're just visiting," Jenna said. "A friend told us about this world, and thought we would enjoy it."

"That's right," Score said, his voice a bit thick. "It's Oracle's fault, not mine. And, so far, I'm not enjoying it."

"Baby," Helaine muttered unsympathetically.

"Well," the woman said, clearly a little confused by what she had been told, "you must of course stay as our guests while you are on our world. I'm sure you'll find it delightful."

"I'm sure you're wrong," Score grumbled.

Pixel paid him no attention. "I'm very curious as to the sort of life you live here," he confessed. "What do you eat? How do you make clothes? How many islands are there? Are they all alike?"

"Trust Pixel to leach all the fun out of everything by trying to turn it into a school lesson," Score complained.

Jenna gave him a withering look. "Aren't you equally fascinated?" she asked him. "This is so different from anything we're used to."

"I just want the ground to stop swaying," Score told her. "Then maybe I can engage my enthusiasm for other things."

The woman had obviously decided to ignore Score's comments, and turned to Pixel with a smile. "We'll be glad to tell you anything that you wish to learn, you poor things. Fancy not living on the sea! Whatever next?" She shook her head in amazement. "Of course, our legends say that we came to this world from another, where our ancestors had been forced to live on dry land, as a punishment from the gods. But our ancestors were rewarded for their good deeds by being brought here and given the bounties of the sea."

"Sounds more like a punishment to me," Score muttered.

"Once you've been here a while," the woman assured him, "you will understand how blessed we are. Everything we need is granted to us by the bounty of the sea. It is everything, and all we need."

Pixel was enthralled. So much to learn here! "The plants," he asked. "How can they live in such salty water? Why doesn't it kill them?"

The woman laughed. "They have special sections of their stems," she explained. "These areas remove the salt from the water, leaving only pure water. The salt nodes fill with salt, and we harvest them. We use the salt for our food. It keeps our fish fresh for us to store, for example. So the plants help us, and we help the plants by removing their excess salt."

"That's amazing," Pixel said. "So, you eat fish and raise plants?"

"We also raise sea wheat," the woman replied. But that can't grow on our island plants." She tapped the leaf below her with her foot. "They need special areas of their own to grow. So our villages have several smaller islands surrounding them where the wheat grows. Our Harvesters then gather the grain for us, and grind it into flour for baking."

"I can't wait to explore all of this," Pixel confessed, rubbing his hands together happily. "Isn't it amazing?" he asked Jenna.

She smiled fondly at him. "It does sound interesting," she agreed. "But I thought that the idea of this vacation was that we just relax?"

Pixel blushed. "I'm sorry, I didn't want to make it sound like you have to investigate everything with me!" he apologized. "It's just that I find it so fascinating, I can't help wanting to explore and see how these people live."

Jenna laughed. "I know. And I'm interested in seeing what herbs and plants they use for medicines. I might be able to find something new here." She scowled at Helaine. "And I'm sure she'd like to find something to butcher."

"Don't start on me," Helaine warned. Her hand went to her hip, but, for once, she wasn't wearing her sword. Score had somehow managed to convince her to leave all her weapons behind. "It's not a vacation if you kill people," he'd said. Helaine had grumbled, but agreed reluctantly. Pixel was pleased—hopefully, Helaine would learn to relax a little on this trip. But not if Jenna started picking fights.

"Why don't you and I go find out about how the natives use their plants?" Pixel suggested quickly to Jenna. "I'm sure Helaine and Score can find something that will amuse them more."

"I was thinking of seeing if I could barf out all of my intestines," Score complained, "or whether I'd only manage my stomach."

"That sounds even less thrilling than studies," Helaine said. "Maybe there's someone here who could show me your fighting techniques?" she asked their host.

The woman looked a little confused. "We do not fight," she said. "We have no reason."

"Well, this isn't a world where you could settle down then, is it?" Jenna sniped. "You'd be out of work."

"I could introduce warfare," Helaine growled. "Starting with you."

Pixel got between the girls again. "Helaine, maybe you could see how they catch their fish?" he suggested. "That's kind of like fighting."

"So is living with her and Jenna," Score muttered. He took Helaine's elbow. "I'll come, too, as long as the lessons don't include catching anything slimy with tentacles."

"Don't worry," Helaine assured him, "Jenna is staying with Pixel."

Ouch! This wasn't working out too well yet, Pixel realized. But it would be unrealistic to expect the two girls to get along too quickly. They needed time to relax. As Score and Helaine were led away by another of the villagers, Pixel heard him saying, "Maybe there's someone here who can give a good massage. I think that would relax even your stiff neck, Helaine."

"I do wish you'd stand up for me against that . . . witch," Jenna complained to Pixel. "You can hear how she's always insulting me."

Pixel swallowed. "It's just her upbringing," he explained. "She can't help herself. You just have to make allowances."

"Yeah, right," Jenna muttered. "It always has to be *me* who makes allowances, not her. You boys are pandering to her delusions of grandeur. She treats both of you like you're beneath her, too, you know."

"We're her friends," Pixel insisted. "She treats us like equals."

"She orders you both around," Jenna insisted. "She's only *pretending* that you're her equals. Haven't you noticed how you always do what she wants?"

As fond as Pixel was of Jenna, this was too much. "This trip was Score's idea," he pointed out. "And Helaine only came along under protest—but that's because she enjoys protesting. I think she and Score are actually very fond of one another."

"Only because he's the rightful King of Ordin," Jenna shot back. "And she sees a chance to become queen. She wants to rule everyone."

For a second, Pixel had a burning image of Eremin. Eremin had been one of the Three Who Rule, despots who had kept the entire Diadem enslaved in their power. Pixel, Score, and Helaine had been stunned to discover that the Three were actually adult versions of themselves, as they might become one day if they were completely corrupted by selfishness and power. Eremin—Helaine's older self—had been an ice-cold, haughty, and murderous witch, used to manipulating other people to her will. Helaine had seen that there was much of Eremin in her own soul, and that one day she might indeed grow up to be her.

It had absolutely terrified her. Ever since then, she'd been working as hard as she could to avoid *ever* being that person. And it had been working, too. Score, for all of his silliness, could somehow manage to make her laugh, and he had also managed to get Helaine to un-bend enough to the point where Pixel strongly suspected she had a crush on him. If she could learn to laugh and love, then there was no way she would ever be Eremin.

However . . . When Jenna was around, it seemed as though Eremin was taking possession of Helaine's soul . . .

There *had* to be a way to get the girls to like one another! Otherwise, the consequences could be quite disastrous—and not just to them, but to the whole Diadem. If Helaine ever did become Eremin, then Pixel wasn't sure that he and Score could ever stand against her.

"Well," their host said, "this *is* a surprising day!" She pointed out to sea. "More visitors!"

Pixel glanced out, and saw distant sails that were heading in this direction. "You don't get a lot of visitors?" he asked.

"Hardly ever," she replied. "And now two lots in one day! The gods of the sea must be smiling on us today!"

For some reason, Pixel felt uneasy. He couldn't imagine why—after all, the woman had said that her people didn't fight. And why should they? The most common reasons wars were fought were to gain land or riches. But there wasn't land as such on this planet—just these floating island villages, carried along by the tides—so there was no reason to fight for those. And as for riches—well, how could people living on the sea ever get gold, or jewels, or anything that anyone else would want to steal? Pixel was sure there was probably minor violence, and maybe even some sort of crimes here—this was hardly likely to be a paradise!—but, on the whole, these folks had been spared wars and battles, which was a wonderful blessing.

So why did that approaching ship worry him?

"Maybe we'd better get back together with Score and Helaine," he said, softly, to Jenna. "Just in case . . ."

Jenna, sensitive as ever, understood. "You believe that ship to be trouble?"

"I don't know," he admitted. "But there's no reason to take a chance, is there? And if there *is* trouble, we'd do well to have Helaine near us."

"Yes," Jenna admitted. "She does have some uses."

Their host had heard this exchange and frowned. "You think there's some kind of a problem?" she asked. "But why would there be? We have done nothing to offend either men or gods."

"Some men don't need an excuse," Pixel muttered. He led the way across the thick leaves to where Score and Helaine were also looking at the approaching sail. Score glanced at Pixel.

"Helaine's spider sense is telling her we're in danger," he said in his usual mocking tones, though he did look concerned. He took Helaine's feelings seriously, because they were her special skill.

"We're in danger from spiders?" Jenna asked, confused.

"No, I just read too many comic books as a kid." As usual, Score's "explanation" didn't explain anything. Jenna obviously had as little clue as to what he meant as Pixel did. Sometimes it was best to ignore Score's comments.

"You feel that there's trouble, also?" Helaine asked Pixel. He nodded, and she glared at Score. "And you convinced me to leave my sword behind!"

"How was I to know there would be trouble?" Score asked, offended. "Oracle assured me this world was quite safe . . ." His voice trailed off. "And, naturally, I believe every word that double-crosser ever utters," he added in disgust.

"Yes," Pixel said. "I suspect he knew there was trouble and carefully neglected to tell us."

"Okay, I'm formally suggesting here that we all put our heads together at the first chance," Score suggested, "and come up with some way that will allow us to beat the crap out of an illusion. He *really* deserves it."

Jenna looked worried. "I could always create a Portal to take us home," she offered.

Helaine gave her a filthy look. "And if we're right, and there is trouble," she growled, "you would have us run away and abandon these people to their fates? That's just the sort of self-centered, cowardly suggestion I'd expect from a *peasant*."

"Girls!" Pixel said hastily, before Jenna could give vent to her fury. "We don't have to fight amongst ourselves—I think we're going to have a real battle on our hands." He gestured out to sea.

The ship was close enough now for them to make out details. It was an old man of war, the type that might be used on Helaine's medieval world, and it was approaching swiftly.

And, snapping in the breeze atop the tallest mast was a flag that didn't need translating. It had a white skull and crossed bones on a black background.

That meant *pirates* on any world!

4

Jenna swallowed hard, and tried to concentrate. She was not a fighter by nature, but a healer, and she really had very little idea what they were to do against a ship full of pirates. She'd heard the stories—mostly from Pixel—of some of the dangers the other three had faced together, but she hadn't really been a part of those. The only time in her life she'd ever really fought was back on Ordin, when she and Pixel had faced the magical ants together and almost died. And they were ants, not people. She didn't know whether she'd ever be able to bring herself to strike another human being. It went against everything she really believed in.

Of course, so did getting herself murdered by pirates.

Her palms were sweating, and she wiped them on her skirt, glancing nervously at the others. Score looked more resigned than anything, as if he was bored with the whole thing. Helaine, naturally, looked like a race horse straining at the gate, eager to be in action. Well, this was just the sort of thing she'd trained for all of her life. And with her naturally vicious nature, she'd be quite happy slaughtering people, Jenna was sure. Pixel—dear, kind Pixel—seemed to be worried, a frown settled on his pretty blue face. He was clenching and unclenching his fist. As if he could sense her fears and worries, he looked at her and smiled slightly. It was very strained, though.

"Don't try fighting physically, if it should come to that," he advised her. "Remember, we are magic users, and have that advantage. Just reach out to your crystals, and find out how to apply the powers that they give you in the best way possible."

"I don't know if I can bring myself to kill anyone," she confessed. "I'm sure I'll let you all down."

"We all try *not* to kill people," Pixel replied. "So that isn't letting us down. Just try and stop them, that's all."

"We'll try talking to them first," Score added. "They may have come here thinking these people were easy targets. They couldn't have expected us to be here. We may be able to persuade them to go away without a fight."

That sounded wonderful to Jenna—at first. "But wouldn't they just go somewhere else, to another island, and attack that instead?" she asked.

"Quite likely," Helaine agreed. She glanced at Score. "Perhaps we should just sink their ship?"

"And strand them here with these innocent farmers?" he said. "I don't think that's any better an idea."

"What would you have us do, then?" Helaine growled.

"What we always do—improvise." Score managed a grin at that. "Play to your strengths, that's what I always say."

"You say too much, as always," Helaine grumbled. But she didn't sound unhappy when she said it.

The pirate ship was quite close now, barely a hundred feet from the edge of the island. To Jenna's surprise, none of the islanders had stopped the work they were doing. Didn't they understand that they were in serious trouble? Then she sighed—no, they probably didn't. It seemed that this kind of thing never happened here.

Until today.

On the ship, pirates were racing about, doing things with the sails to make them smaller. Jenna realized that this meant the wind wouldn't push the ship along as fast, so it was a way of bringing the ship to a halt. On the front of the ship were men with grappling hooks, swinging them and then throwing them. The hooks bit into the thick leaves, and then the ropes went taut. In moments, the ship was resting beside the island, and the pirates rushed to the side. They had swords and scythes and some had bows and arrows.

One of them—obviously their leader—jumped up onto the side wall of the ship, and gripped a rope with one hand, his other brandishing a large, curved sword. He was dressed in dark clothes, with a red sash about his waist, and another about his head. He had a thick, dark beard and nasty eyes. "On the island!" he called. "Stop your work immediately, and come aboard!"

The woman who had been their host looked confused, but no one else paid any attention. "Surely you know we can't do that?" the woman called back. "We have our tasks to do—such as making the meals for our Harvesters for when they return."

"They won't be returning, fool," the man snarled. "They're already in our hold, where you'll be joining them. Come aboard, I say, or we'll be forced to damage some of you." He gestured, and the pirates with bows got ready to fire.

Jenna was now scared for these kind islanders. They would be captured or killed, because they knew even less about fighting than she did. She couldn't allow that to happen! She reached into the pouch tied to her waist for her four jewels. Pixel had said to rely on her powers that these jewels amplified, so she touched them with her fingers and her mind. Carnelian, for healing. No, that wouldn't help yet. Obsidian—invisibility! That was better! If she made herself invisible, then the pirates couldn't hurt her. But that wouldn't help much in a fight, unless she went about invisibly and tripped pirates up, or something . . . Citrine, for persuasion . . . That could help, if she could somehow persuade the pirates to go away. But that would only work for a short while, and then they'd either come back again or else strike somewhere else. Finally, there was aquamarine, for survival. She wasn't entirely sure what that might mean—she'd read the description in The Book of Magic—but it sounded like something that would help only her.

What was the good of having magic powers and gems if they didn't help out?

Helaine wasn't having those problems. She stepped forward. "Surrender now," she suggested. "It'll save you a lot of pain in the long run."

The pirate captain looked at her in astonishment, and then laughed. "Well, I needed my joke of the day," he gasped. "And you just gave it to me, girlie. I may make you the ship's fool when you're our captive."

"You're the fool, not me," Helaine answered coldly.

"Getting her mad," Score said. "Not a good idea. Okay, she doesn't have a sword, but—"

"Who says I don't?" Jenna could feel Helaine's use of magic, and then almost smiled as a sword leaped from the startled fingers of one of the pirates and flew into Helaine's hand. Of course—she'd used her sapphire to levitate it. Helaine whirled the sword once, and then smiled grimly. "Wanna fight?"

The captain looked confused, and then angry. "Kill a few," he snarled to his men. "Especially her. But not too many—we want slaves, remember."

The archers targeted their bows to let fly.

Jenna didn't know what to do, but, almost by instinct, she reached out to the obsidian. She had made the four of them invisible. The archers hesitated, but simply moved their aim toward the islanders. There was a *zing* as loud as a strong wind as the archers let their arrows fly. Jenna felt Score using his emerald for transformation, and all of the arrows vanished in puffs of smoke. Jenna was thrilled—the islanders were safe!

"Make us visible again," Helaine ordered. "I can't see my limbs, and I can't fight if I can't see myself." That was typical of her, just issuing commands.

Pixel added: "We have to make them target us, not the innocents here. It was a good move, but we can't use it right now."

That was different. Jenna brought down her invisibility barrier, and the pirates gasped. The captain yelled: "It's just a trick!"

"They're sorcerers," one of his men called out in fear. The captain slapped the man hard across the face, knocking him down.

"They're trying to trick us, is all. We know there are no magic users on this world. They're just kids—take them!"

Jenna was confused—the man talked like he and his men weren't from this planet. What could that mean? But they would have to find out later—right now, pirates were jumping over the side of the ship onto the floating island. Some of them headed toward the confused islanders, who had finally stopped working to watch what was happening. A bunch of the raiders headed for the four of them, though.

Helaine laughed happily, and jumped forward. She swung her stolen sword easily, catching the attack of the first pirate who tried to simply run through her. She turned the blow aside, and used the hilt of the sword to hit him across the temple. Stunned, he fell at her feet, and she moved on to face the next one.

Score was working differently. Using his powers of transformation, he was doing all sorts of really silly things to stop pirates. He was making bowls of laughing gas appear around their heads; he was tossing sticky food substances into their faces, blinding them; he was dissolving bits of leaves beneath their feet, making them stumble. It was almost as if he wasn't taking the whole thing seriously, which was so typical of him.

Pixel was using his topaz, which gave him power over fire. He was having to be careful, of course, since most of the island was made up of flammable dried plant products, but he was shooting thin streams of fire that burned bow strings, or heated swords so that their owners had to drop them. He was quite focused, and she was proud of him.

She wished that there was something that she could do to help, but her own abilities were mostly gentle ones. Then she saw a pirate slip and fall, and she had an idea. Instead of using her invisibility on herself, she started to use it on things about them. She made a thick root vanish from in front of one pirate, and he tripped over it. She made sections of the leaves seem to vanish, leaving pits down to the ocean below. The scared pirates didn't know if it was a trick, or one of Score's real pits, so they had to avoid them anyway. She made one pirate's legs vanish. He screamed, thinking he'd been injured, and then floundered around, unable to keep his balance. All she could do were tricks, of course, but they all slowed down the attackers.

By now, the villagers had realized that they were in serious trouble. Since they weren't fighters, they did the most sensible thing, which was to run away as far and as fast as possible.

It was hard for Jenna to think, because the fight was so confusing. She was mostly aware of it as separate small sights and sounds—Helaine laughing as she went sword to sword with a pirate; Score howling as he threw a custard pie into the face of another; Pixel scowling as he directed a stream of fire at another pirate's pants. It wasn't making sense, but she supposed that would come later.

A large pirate rushed toward her, raising a long knife, ready to strike her. She gasped and dodged aside, making herself invisible as she stumbled. It was hard to keep your balance when you couldn't see yourself!

"I know you're there somewhere, girl," the man snarled, hacking out with his sword. He was getting perilously close to her!

Jenna wished that she was more used to fighting, and then realized how terrible that idea was—as if she *wanted* to fight! But she did need more skill at it, because she didn't really know what to do. Make the sword invisible, so the pirate couldn't see what he was using to attack her? But then *she* wouldn't be able to see where it was, either! No, she had to do something else . . . She touched the citrine, and then said, softly and sincerely: "You've already killed me. I'm dead. I'm not worth bothering about."

The pirate abruptly looked puzzled, and then shrugged, turning away. "What am I doing?" he muttered to himself. "She's already dead. I must be losing my mind." He ran off, looking for another victim.

For a second, Jenna was elated—now she could deal with the pirates without getting hurt! And then she realized how futile her idea was as she looked around.

Helaine had managed to wound several of the pirates, putting them out of action. Score had knocked out or winded a bunch more, and Pixel seemed to have dealt with a fair number himself. But there were always more, and her having sent one pirate running was hardly contributing to the battle. Plus, several of the raiders had made it past the four magic users, and were attacking the villagers. They weren't trying to kill them, just capture them, which was very strange. Jenna had always believed that pirates took what they wanted in loot, not people. But, of course, the islanders didn't have very much to loot.

So why were the pirates attacking them in the first place?

This was the time for action, though, not thought. She had to do something to stop the pirates, and the citrine seemed to be her best shot at it. She concentrated hard, as hard as she could, and then sent her whisperings out to the pirates who were trying to capture the islanders. "You have all the captives you need," she told the attackers. "You don't need these. Let them go, and return to your ship. Let them go."

It was taking a lot of her strength to project this message. Pixel had explained that the farther out from the center of the Diadem they went, the weaker their magic was. Brine was on the Outer Rim, so their powers were at their weakest here. It was taking all of her concentration and most of her bodily strength to project her message to so many people and make them believe it. But it was working. The pirates stopped going after the villagers, and instead started rounding up imaginary captives and bustling them back to the ship. Jenna grinned at her success—at last, she was contributing something useful!

Then there came a heavy blow across the back of her neck. She stumbled to her knees, her entire back a flame of pain. She had to struggle to simply stay conscious, but she managed to glance back over her burning shoulder. One of the pirates was behind her, and had struck her with a pike he was carrying.

"Blasted witch!" he spat. "Making them believe un-truths! You'll pay for that!" He slammed the pike down again, hard, across her left arm. More pain lanced through her, and Jenna almost lost her feeble grip on her awareness.

"No killing!" the pirate captain roared. "Take them alive, you dogs!"

The pirate attacking her hesitated for a moment, then cursed under his breath. He reached down and scooped Jenna up almost effortlessly, and slung her across his shoulder. Jenna couldn't fight through the pain to concentrate on any magic. It was all she could do to hang on and watch. Lolling over his shoulder, she saw only snatches of sights that didn't mean much. Then the pirate swung back aboard his ship, and threw her to the deck.

Hitting the deck made the pain worse. But some-how she staggered into a sitting position, and looked back at the island. Her spell had held together, even through her pain, and many of the pirates were re-turning to the ship empty-handed, but thinking they were driving captives. Some pirates, however, really did have slaves, and they were being thrust onto the deck. The captain was back aboard, and directing the grapples to be loosened, and the sails set.

"Magic users!" he spat, furiously. "We can't fight them with swords. Get the fire pots ready!"

His men rushed to obey, carrying cauldrons from which flames danced—obviously some sort of combustible material. The captain directed the men, and they poured the liquid fire over the side and onto the broad, thick leaves of the island. Immediately, the dry vegetation caught fire, and the flames started to spread.

"Back to the ship!" he called to his men, and those who were able retreated. A few couldn't, and were abandoned.

Jenna saw Pixel leap into action. With his topaz, he tried to douse the flames that were spreading. She realized that the whole island might burn down if the fire was unchecked. And if it did, then there was nowhere that the islanders could go. Trust Pixel to risk his life so nobly to save others!

But he was too focused on what he was doing. As he fought the fires, one of the retreating pirates managed to catch him by surprise. Jenna gasped as the sword blade slammed into Pixel's head, and he stumbled and fell. The pirate grabbed him, and threw him up to eager arms on the ship. Pixel was hoisted aboard, and dumped beside her. Then the ship rolled away from the island as the last remaining attackers jumped aboard. With a billow of sails, the ship moved off, crashing through the waves.

Jenna examined Pixel. There was a gash in his forehead that was bleeding badly, and he was unconscious. She knew she would be able to heal him with her powers—except she was still too weak to use magic. And her own pain was almost too much to take. Her strength was gone, and blackness overtook her.

5

Score saw the flames burst as the pirates covered their retreat. Thick smoke belched from the leaves as they caught fire. Some sort of napalm, he guessed, and one that made the fires spread quickly. Though the island floated on the sea, the inhabited parts were quite dry, and were igniting fast.

There was no time to waste. He gripped his chrysolite, and reached out with his ability to affect water. It took most of his strength, but he created a small whirlpool of water, stretching it into a water spout. He then brought this crashing down on the flames. Steam sizzled, leaves cracked, and a wave of hot air wafted over him, but the fire was out. Only a small portion of the island had been consumed, and he assumed that the natives would be able to grow this back eventually.

The pirate ship was already nearly a mile away, and making good time with the prevailing winds helping it along.

Helaine was beside him, clutching her sword in fury. "They're getting away!" she snarled.

"And faster than we could chase them," he agreed, rather smugly. "But we beat them, and they didn't get what they were after." He frowned. "Which was people, and that's odd. I thought pirates went after treasure."

"Maybe here the treasure *is* people," Helaine suggested. "But they'll just strike somewhere else now, find some other island. We should have sunk their ship."

"And then done what with the pirates?" Score asked her. "We couldn't leave them here—these islanders are as helpless as sheep. As it is, I don't know what we'll do with the pirates that were left behind." He counted the fallen. "Six of them . . . Four badly wounded, that are going to need care."

"We should feed them to the sharks," Helaine suggested. "It's all they're good for, attacking unarmed people."

"I hope Jenna doesn't hear that," Score muttered, looking around. "Hey, where is Jenna? And Pixel, come to that? I can't see them."

Helaine scanned the island. "Nor can I. That's odd."

The woman who had been their host earlier approached them. She was still shaking from fear. Most of the natives had retreated and watched the battle from afar. "Thank you for saving us," she said. "And I am sorry about your friends."

"Sorry?" Score stared at her. "What do you mean?"

"Didn't you see what happened to them during the battle?" the woman asked.

"We were rather busy," Helaine snapped. "Fighting to save you. What happened to them?"

"They were both captured, and taken onto the ship."

Score was stunned. He almost felt like screaming. "Taken?" he repeated, numbly.

"Those pigs have our friends?" Helaine growled. "We must go after them," she decided, immediately. "Pixel and Jenna must be recovered, and their captors punished."

"Whoa," Score said, grabbing her shoulder. "We need to plan for it. And, anyway, I thought you'd be glad to be rid of Jenna."

Helaine flushed. "I am thinking only of Pixel," she replied.

"Right, mentioning her name was a slip of the lips." Score managed a wan grin. "I promise not to tell her you were worried about her."

"I am *not* worried about her," Helaine said firmly.

"Well, there's probably no real need to be," Score said. "She and Pixel can handle themselves."

"She is a novice at fighting," Helaine pointed out. "And she is too gentle to attempt to really hurt anyone."

"You say that like it's a bad thing."

"When lives are threatened, being gentle is fatal," Helaine said. "Force is the only answer."

"It's never the only answer," Score contradicted her gently. "Especially for us, since we have magic."

"We need to stop talking and go after them," Helaine insisted.

"We'll never catch that ship," Score pointed out. "So we need to know where they are going. Now I actually feel glad we've got a few of these scum as prisoners." He turned to their host. "Four of these pirates need medical attention. Can your people deal with that?"

The woman scowled. "They are our enemies. They tried to kidnap or kill us. Why should we help them at all? We should feed them to the fish."

Helaine scowled at the woman, and brought her sword up to threaten her. "They are human beings in need. You will help them, or answer to me." The woman paled and rushed off to recruit help.

Score looked at her with some affection. "Weren't you the one just suggesting their use as shark kibble?" he asked her.

"I was merely venting," Helaine replied with dignity.

"I knew that." Score patted her shoulder. "I'm proud of you; one day, you'll become a real girl, Pinnochio."

"Half the time, I do not know what you're talking about," Helaine complained, but there was a slight lift to the edge of her lips. Score thought it looked kind of nice on her.

"No surprise," he replied. "Half the time, I don't know what I'm talking about, either." Having dealt with the injured, he turned his attention to the remaining two pirates. One was unconscious still, having suffered a blow to the head from Helaine's sword hilt. The other was awake and looking like a caged wolf. If there was anywhere for him to bolt to, he'd have run. But on a small island, where could he flee? There was fear and hatred in his eyes, and that cheered Score up. "Right," he told the man, "you're going to tell us what we want to know."

"I'll tell ye nothing," the man answered surlily.

"Oh, I'm sure you'll reconsider that," Score said, smiling. He looked at Helaine, and hoped she understood the concept of good cop/bad cop. She might be from a medieval world, but there was absolutely nothing backward about her mind.

Helaine looked thoughtful. "Do you have any idea," she asked Score, "how many fingers a man could loose before he bled to death?"

"No, I don't," Score replied.

"How about a little experiment?" Helaine suggested, eyeing their prisoner. He had gone pale.

"Ye wouldn't," he gasped.

"She *needn't*," Score replied. "If you give us a few simple answers. Think of it like a game show—you give the correct answer, you get to keep a finger."

The pirate stared at him, and then at Helaine, who was testing the edge of her blade. "If I tell ye anything, Black Hawk will kill me," he protested.

"You've *already* told us something," Score replied. "Now we know the name of your boss, don't we? Anyway, look on the bright side. If you tell us what you know, Black Hawk will only kill you if he first beats us—which isn't very likely. Then if we tell him that you told us—which we wouldn't, if you're nice and cooperative—and then if he can find his way back here, which I'm sure he can't. So it's not really very likely he'll do anything to you. On the other hand . . ." He gave Helaine a long, hard look. "*She's* here, she's got a sword, and a really short temper. If you're nice to me, *maybe* I can persuade her not to hurt you. I can't *guarantee* it, because she doesn't listen to anyone when the berserker rage is on her . . ."

The pirate seemed to be caught midway in his decision. "She's just a girl," he protested. "She'd faint at the sight of blood."

"That does it," Helaine announced. "It's time to start losing digits." She whirled the sword around. "If you stand *very* still, I'm sure I'll be able to only hit what I'm aiming at. Move, and you might lose more than I expect." She did a fast spin and the sword flickered out.

A bright red gash opened on the man's left cheek. It started to drip blood down his face. He screamed, more in fear than pain, Score thought.

71

"As you can see," Helaine said, "I don't faint at the sight of blood. Or, I might add, severed body parts . . . Now, the other cheek, then I'll start on the fingers . . ."

"Stop her," the pirate begged Score, clutching at his cheek.

"You know how to stop her," Score answered, feeling a little queasy, but trying to sound determined. "Black Hawk took two of our friends, and some people we're protecting. If we don't get them back, she's liable to be a little cranky, and she'll take it out on you."

"Stand still," Helaine ordered the man. "If you keep trembling like that, I might cut your ear off instead of just slicing your cheek." She looked more cheerful. "Come to think of it, you don't really *need* two ears, do you?" She took up her stance again, sword in hand, eyeing his right ear.

"Stop her!" the pirate screamed. "I'll tell you what you want to know!"

Helaine scowled. "You're just saying that to annoy me," she complained. "Score, how do we even know he'll tell us the truth?"

"Because if he doesn't, he knows we'll be back—and that you'll be even more mad." He grinned. "Then you'd probably take his fingers off one joint at a time . . ."

"It's the truth, I swear it!" the pirate promised, trembling. He was obviously thoroughly terrified of Helaine's "madness." "Just keep her away from me."

"Talk," Score ordered.

"I don't know much," the man said.

"That does it," Helaine growled. "He's just playing around. Ear next."

"No!" he screamed, covering his ears hastily. "I mean, I'm just a deck hand—I don't know a whole lot. I just do what I'm told. I probably don't know most of the answers you want."

"Then tell me what you *do* know," Score said. "And I'll judge if it's enough to allow you to keep a few fingers. You could probably get by with two on each hand . . ."

"Black Hawk is the one you really want," the pirate blubbered. "He started it all. I was just a Harvester once. You probably don't know, but it's really boring work. Black Hawk came in his ship and offered us men a chance to get some excitement, and I jumped at the offer."

"Helping terrorize and kidnap other people," Helaine growled. "You make me sick."

"It's just a job," the pirate protested weakly. "Black Hawk built up quite a gang. He has two other ships out like ours, capturing people, so he needed fresh crews. If anyone didn't agree to join him, then he took them as slaves. I didn't want to be a slave."

"So you helped him get others," Score said. "Wonderful. Okay, what happens to the slaves?"

"I don't know." The pirate saw Helaine tighten her grip on the sword, and almost fainted. "I swear, I don't know why Black Hawk wants them! We just take whoever we've caught to an island, and leave them there. There's a town of some sort on the island, and more of his men there. They take the slaves, and we sail off for more."

Score sighed. "I wish Pixel was here—he'd probably have this whole business worked out by now. But I think it's clear that the pirates are running a slave camp on the island for some reason."

"I think they're digging for treasure," their captive said quickly. "They're taken into what looks like an area of caves near the volcano."

Helaine shrugged. "It's possible, I suppose. Maybe a diamond mine, or something? Black Hawk wants slaves to dig for him, because he doesn't want to do the work himself?"

"I don't know," Score said miserably. He really *was* missing Pixel—the blue boy had a sharper mind than anyone he knew. "It doesn't make a lot of sense to me. Treasure is only treasure if you can spend it—and what is there to spend diamonds on here?" He shrugged. "Still, that must be where Pix and Jenna will be taken, so we have to go there too." He looked at the pirate. "How do we get there?"

"I don't know."

"This is getting monotonous," Helaine complained. "Hold his hand out."

"I don't know!" the man screamed. "I'm just a deck hand and pirate! I don't know how to navigate at sea! I can't tell you how to get to the island!"

"Come to think of it, I can't navigate at sea, either," Score said. "So even if he told us, it wouldn't help us get there. Now what?"

"I could just chop bits off him anyway," Helaine said, sounding hopeful. "It might jog his memory."

Several of the islanders had been listening to what they were doing. They weren't interfering, and most of them looked as afraid of Helaine as the pirate did. One of the younger men stepped forward.

"I think I can help," he offered. "There aren't many islands, and I do know where some are." He grinned, rather bashfully. "When I was a teen, I got bored of being a worker, too. I took off in a boat to see what was out there in the world. I'm an excellent sailor."

"That sounds useful," Score replied, cheering up a bit. "Do you think you can find this island he told us about?"

"I only know of one that's not too far away with a volcano and caves that might be turned into mines." He looked at the captive. "Is the island shaped like a half-moon, with a coral reef filling in the rest of the curve? And does it have a large bite out of it to the east, where a ship can anchor?"

"Yes," the pirate said. "That's it, exactly! And the sands are sort of reddish. There's a big stand of cheppa trees near the harbor."

The islander nodded. "Then I know the place." He turned back to Score and Helaine. "I am certain I can take you there."

"Okay!" Score said, happily. "A plan! Maybe we don't need Pixel as much as I thought."

"We're still getting him back," Helaine insisted. "And Jenna, too, I suppose. Though I can always hope that the pirates have killed her because she's so annoying . . ."

"Ah . . ." the islander said. "There is one small problem, though. We don't have any boats."

"Huh?" Score was confused. "I thought you guys had lots of them?"

"The Harvesters use most of them," the man apologized. "And the pirates captured them, and left their boats out at the sea-wheat islands. We only had a couple here, and they were both burned by the pirates."

"Great," Score muttered. "So now we know where the pirates' lair is, but we just can't get there."

"You give in too easily," Helaine complained. "There must be a way for us to get there." She considered for a moment. "I could use my sapphire to levitate us," she suggested.

"Three of us?" Score asked. "And we're on a Rim World, don't forget, so your power isn't as great as usual. And there aren't a lot of places for us to rest, unless you feel like swimming."

"That would not be a good idea out at sea," the islander said. "There are creatures out there that would eat you—even if you do have strange, magical powers."

"Wonderful." Score's hopes sank again. "So now what do we do?"

6

Helaine glared at Score, angrily. Honestly, some times he could be a real pain! She had an almost overwhelming temptation to punch him, but restrained herself. That would not be a good move, no matter how much she might enjoy it on one level. "Stop feeling sorry for yourself," she ordered. "Pixel and Jenna need our help, and there must be some way to get to them. Put your mind to it, and think of a way!"

Score gave her a mock curtsy. "Yes, your majesty," he replied. "Any other miracles you'd like me to attempt at the same time?"

Her face went warm. "Yes, you might try curbing your sarcasm—and that *would* be a miracle!"

"Yeah, you're probably right—I'd have a better chance at getting the sun to stop in the sky." He brooded for a moment. "I just need inspiration, that's all. I'm sure it'll come to me . . ." He appeared to be deep in thought.

Their new friend looked at her in confusion. "You can do magic," he protested. "Surely this task is simple for you?"

"Not so simple," Helaine answered. "We each have certain abilities that are stronger. For example, I can shape-shift using my onyx. Score can't do that as easily as I can—it would take a lot of energy out of him, even if he could manage it. For me, it's quite simple." She broke off, grinning. "Score! How about I shape-shift into something that can swim or fly? Something big enough to carry both of you?"

Score patted her rather condescendingly on the arm. "Good try, bad idea."

"Why?" she demanded. "Because it's mine?"

"No. You just haven't thought it through. Okay, let's say you become a whale, and we can sit on your back. There are nasty beasties out there in this sea that might like to snack on whales. As for turning into—oh, a flying dragon . . . Two problems. First, do you *know* how to fly? I mean, it takes birds a while to figure it out, so I imagine it's not so simple. Second, how long would you be able to fly before you needed to rest? And there's nowhere to rest on an empty ocean." He gave her a thin smile. "As I said, nice try, but it won't work. You're on the right lines, though— it has to involve our magic somehow . . ."

Much as she hated to admit it, Helaine realized that Score's objections were valid. Okay, so what about her other gems? Sapphire for levitation—no, they already knew that wouldn't last. Agate—communications. She couldn't see any way that would help. And her chryso-prase gave her power over earth—in a place where there was just water everywhere! She felt so useless. It was up to Score to figure out a way to accomplish this rescue, but he seemed to be out of ideas—except for ones about her in barely any clothing . . .

"It seems as if all you can do right now is to think of girls in bikinis," she complained. "Can't you be more useful?"

"Spoilsport . . ." Then he brightened again. "Helaine, you're a genius! You got me thinking the right way after all! Babes in bikinis *can* be a bright idea," he grinned. "There's this James Bond movie with a girl in a bikini, and she collects seashells. That's what we need—a huge seashell." Abruptly, he kissed the end of her nose. "See—even when you complain, you inspire me."

Helaine found herself blushing, and didn't know why. "A huge shell?" she asked.

"A huge seashell?" the islander repeated. "We do not have any larger than . . ." He held the thumbs and middle fingers of each hand together. "About that."

"Doesn't matter," Score assured him. "One of my powers is the changing of size. I can make things bigger or smaller." He looked thoughtful for a moment, then shook his head and carried on. "I can grow the shell to as big as we need it to carry the three of us and some supplies. Then Helaine can propel it with her levitation. And if she gets tired, I have the power over water, so I can drive it along using waves or something. And because it's a shell, it'll be like armor, so none of the nasties in the sea should be able to hurt us."

Helaine grinned. "I *knew* you'd work out a plan," she said.

"You were right," he replied. "I just needed the right motivation. You in a bikini . . . Mmmm!"

"You're going to keep saying that all day, aren't you?" Helaine complained.

"Maybe not. But I will be *thinking* it."

Helaine didn't doubt that for a moment.

Shanara studied Oracle suspiciously. She was in her castle lair, with her experiments in magic all about her, and her companion, Blink, snoozing on his perch. She had used her scrying bowl to see what was happening to her four young friends, and had seen Pixel and Jenna captured. Oracle didn't appear to be very worried.

"Don't you think you could be more help?" she finally asked him.

He spread his hands. "How?"

"You might have told them everything you know about that world," she pointed out.

Oracle shrugged. "I might have told them everything about *everything* I know," he pointed out. "But would that really help them? It would clutter their heads with a lot of useless information. No, I'm sure they'll be able to learn what they need without too much prompting from me."

"You've sent them into a potentially very dangerous situation," Shanara snapped, "and you've deliberately kept back information that might help them."

"*We've* sent them," Oracle corrected her. "You had a hand in it, don't forget. And you know the same information as I do, so you could have told them. Why didn't you?"

Shanara squirmed slightly. "I didn't know it all when we sent them off," she said. "And I'm sure there's still a lot that you know and I don't."

Oracle smiled lazily. "Yes, I think that's fair to say."

"Then why won't you help them?"

Oracle suddenly looked quite serious. "Shanara, they're teenagers. For one thing, they don't like to be *told* everything—they like to discover it for themselves. Yes, certainly, I could have sat all four of them down before they went off and filled their heads with lots of information. They'd have been bored stupid, and wouldn't have heard half of what I said. This way, discovering it for themselves, they'll remember it all."

"Is that your only excuse?" she asked him.

"No," he admitted. "There's one even more important. They are potentially the most powerful magicians in the Diadem. Not now, certainly, but in ten or twenty years it's very unlikely there will be anyone about to match them."

Shanara nodded. "I'll grant you that. They have wonderful potential."

"Wonderful—and terrible," Oracle corrected her. "Don't forget that they once grew up to be the Three Who Rule. It isn't beyond all possibilities that they may yet become those evil people once again."

"Never," Shanara said firmly. "Their hearts are too pure for that."

"Really?" Oracle crossed his arms and stared at her. "Helaine is getting awfully like Eremin at times, isn't she? Especially around Jenna. Who, I might add, was *your* idea. 'Get another girl, make them four, and they'll never be the Three Who Rule.' I assume you recall saying that?"

"You agreed with me at the time, as I remember it."

"In hindsight, perhaps a mistake. Jenna is pushing Helaine toward Eremin, and you know it."

Shanara felt like screaming, but it would have shown Oracle how much he was getting under her skin, and she would never do that. "It's purely temporary. Helaine has a good heart, and Jenna is a sweet girl. Sooner or later, they *must* become friends."

"Why? Because you wish it?" Oracle laughed. "Love is beyond even *your* powers, Shanara, no matter how much of an illusion it might be at times. And Jenna and Helaine are highly unlikely to bend sufficiently to even tolerate one another, let alone actually get to like one another."

"It will happen," Shanara said, stubbornly. She knew it was more wish than fact, but she would not give in.

"Perhaps. But my point is that we have to let the four of them make their own mistakes from time to time, even if it endangers them. Their discovery of further evil in the Diadem will cement their determination to fight it, not to succumb to it. If they fight evil in others, they will not allow it in themselves."

"We do not *know* that," Shanara argued.

"There's too much we don't know," Oracle agreed. "If only our magic could penetrate the past, and allow us to discover what caused the Three Who Rule to become the way they were! But they covered their tracks far too well when they were hiding from Sarman, and *nothing* can get us past that barrier." He tried to punch the wall, but his hand went right through it, since he was just an illusion. "Maybe loving Jenna will prevent

Pixel from becoming Nantor—but maybe she's the trigger that will turn him into Nantor."

"How?" asked Shanara, scowling. "She's a sweet, loving child, and would never allow Pixel to become so bitter and murderous as Nantor was."

Oracle gestured at the scrying bowl. "We just saw that she's been captured by the pirates. What if they kill her? It might drive Pixel mad with grief, and turn him into Nantor. The problem is that we don't know! We're working in the dark here, fighting a war with the three of them that they don't even have a clue is going on!"

"We're not fighting them—we're protecting them," Shanara protested.

"It amounts to the same thing in the end," Oracle pointed out. "Protecting or fighting, we have to ensure that they *never* become the Three. And I hope that you're totally committed to that end."

Shanara couldn't help disliking Oracle at times, and this was certainly one of them. "You *know* I am, you wretched illusion! You know that I, above all, have the most to fear if they ever become the Three Who Rule. They'd only dissolve you, and murder and enslave worlds. But if they ever find out who I *really*

am, and come after me, I won't ever get off so lightly."
She shuddered, and tried to repress her terrible memories again. But she knew she would have the night-
mares again tonight, as she so often did.

Oracle had the grace to look ashamed. It was probably another one of his acts, but she appreciated the
gesture. "You're quite right," he said gently. "You have
more to lose than anyone. I wouldn't have brought up
the point, but it's much too vital to leave unspoken."
He stared at her intently. "If the worst should happen,
then—are you prepared to kill them?"

Shanara had hoped he would never ask that, and
always knew he was bound to do so. She had to look
deep within herself for this. Score, Pixel, and Helaine
were three wonderful children—well, teens now, really, and growing fast. She loved their company and delighted in their antics.

And was terrified of their potential.

There was only one possible answer. "Yes," she said
softly. "Yes, if it becomes necessary, I *can* kill them." A
tear trickled down her cheek. She knew Oracle would
wonder if it was real or an illusion, but saw no need to
tell him. "Trust you to leave me to do your dirty work—
since there's no way you could do the deed yourself."

"Actually, there is," Oracle replied. "I know I'm not strictly real—but, in the same sense, neither is magic itself."

"You're a creature of magic!" Shanara protested. "You can't perform magic yourself!"

"True—but I don't need to actually be able to do it myself." Oracle looked pensive. "I never need sleep, and I rarely stay in one place long. I've taken to wandering the worlds, observing and learning. That's how I discovered what's going on on Brine. Well, another of my journeys took me to another world, and there . . ." He shuddered. "There I found something that even the Three couldn't defeat. If I need to kill them, all I have to do is to lure them to that world."

"And which world might that be?"

Oracle shook his head. "No, I won't tell you. Trust me, it's knowledge you do not need. And you've already seen enough horrors in your life. I'll spare you this one."

Shanara nodded. He was right. Then she hugged herself and sighed. "Some friends we are," she muttered. "Those kids are in trouble, and here we are, planning their deaths . . ."

"We *are* their friends!" Oracle said harshly. "Don't you think the three of them would rather be dead than become the Three?"

Shanara considered it a moment. "Yes. Right now, they would. But the change may very well be gradual. Are you certain we'll be able to spot the point where they are inevitably bound to become the Three if it happens?"

"No," Oracle admitted. "No, I'm not. But we have to be ever-watchful and ever-alert. If we even have the slightest suspicion of their turning—then we must strike. They're already so powerful that we would never get a second chance. We have to kill them on the first attempt."

Another tear trickled down her cheek. Shanara sighed again. "Oh, Oracle, what have we become?"

"Possibly the last chance the Diadem has," he replied. "Don't ever forget that. The only reason we have a chance of killing Score, Helaine, and Pixel is because they trust us completely—and we have to make sure they never lose that trust. It's our greatest weapon against them, should we ever need it."

Shanara nodded. But she felt very unclean, and there was no way to remove this stain from her soul . . .

7

Pixel struggled to wake, as though he were drowning in a deep lake. He had the vague impression that there was someone talking to him, and that there was pain in his head, but it was terribly hard for him to focus. He knew, though, that he had to make the effort, that there was a very important reason for him to do so.

Finally, he was able to open his eyes weakly. There wasn't much light, and his vision was all blurry, but there was no way he could mistake Jenna's face hovering uncertainly in his sight. Then he was able to make some sense out of what she was saying.

"Pixel," she repeated. "Wake—and stay awake. You've had a bad blow to the head. If you fall unconscious again, you may never wake up. Do you understand me?"

"No," he admitted. The words were clear enough, but his mind refused to make them mean much of anything. His voice was dry and raspy. He felt something wet at his lips.

"Drink this," Jenna ordered him. "Sip it slowly. It's just water."

Pixel tried, but his throat refused to swallow, and he felt the water dribble back out of his mouth again. What had happened to him? Where was he? What was going on? He couldn't remember anything, really, except that the sweet face he was looking at belonged to Jenna.

"Don't try talking," she instructed him. "I guess your mind is still a bit shook up. A pirate attacked you and hit you on the forehead. Do you remember that?"

Again, he heard the words, but it was so dreadfully hard to give them any meaning. He did get the idea that he'd been hurt, and that made sense. Since his head felt like it was on fire, that must be where he'd been hit. But he couldn't remember it. He tried to reach up with his hand to touch his forehead, but Jenna gently prevented this.

"No, don't touch it. I'm trying to heal it, but without my herbs and poultices, I'm not doing too well. I've been using my carnelian, and that's helped to close the wound. But it might be infected, and I need my potions to cure that."

Oh. He was hurt. Yes, he could understand that. He wished he could think straight. Maybe this would all make sense later. He wanted to go back to sleep again, but Jenna refused to allow this.

"You have to stay awake!" she cried urgently. "If you don't, you may go into a coma. Do you understand?"

"No," he managed to croak. "Don't understand anything . . ."

A second girl moved into view and looked down at him. She didn't look familiar—but, right now, nothing much did. "Is he going to die?"

"No!" Jenna said, desperately, firmly. "I'm using all my powers to make sure that he doesn't. But I'm worried about him—he seems very sick. His brain may have been affected by the blow."

His brain? That seemed to be important. Pixel knew that he had a very sharp brain, one that could solve problems so simply, when others were confused. But if something had happened to his brain, he'd be *nothing*. It had to start working properly again! Maybe after he had a little nap he'd feel better . . .

Cruelly, Jenna shook him back awake. "Pixel, don't! You *have* to stay awake! Please! For me!"

"Okay," he murmured, hoping she'd shut up so he could sleep.

The other girl looked worried. "Jenna, Munson is sick again, also. Can you look at him? I'm afraid he might die."

"I'm busy," Jenna growled.

"Jenna, *please!*" the girl begged. "There's nobody else here who knows medicine, and the pirates will just let him die. I'll sit here with Pixel, and keep him awake until you get back, I promise. But you have to help us! Nobody else can or will."

Jenna looked worried, and Pixel wished he could cheer her up. Yes, help others—that's what they had to do with their powers. They couldn't be selfish and just look after themselves. Otherwise . . . otherwise what? He couldn't remember, but he knew it was something bad. He tried to tell Jenna to go and look after this other person, and that he'd be fine, especially if she let him snooze a while. But his words all came out mumbled and jumbled, and he didn't think she understood.

Still, Jenna finally stood up. "All right," she agreed reluctantly. "I can't let him suffer. But be certain that you stay here with Pixel. Don't let him fall asleep, even if you have to slap him. And call out if he gets worse, okay?"

The girl nodded and slipped in beside Pixel. Jenna took a last look, and then fled from his sight. He tried to focus on the other girl. He knew a name from somewhere—Helaine—but he didn't know if this was her. He tried to ask, but again his words just spilled out in an odd order.

"It's all right, Pixel," the girl said. "I'll stay with you. Maybe talking to you is the best idea. If you can hear me, it might help you understand. Right, first of all, my name is Lahra."

Oh! Not Helaine, then. He wondered who Helaine was. Then he wondered if he knew Lahra. She looked quite pretty.

"Pirates attacked my Harvesting party and took us all captive. Munson was hurt. Your friend Jenna has gone off to try and help him. Well, after attacking us, they went on to attack our village. I couldn't see what happened—we're in the ship's hold, and there aren't any windows, or anything—but they caught a few more people, including you and Jenna. You had this horrible gash in your head, and you were bleeding all over the place. I thought you were dead, but you aren't—at least, not yet. Jenna says she's sure she can save you, and I hope she's right."

So do I, thought Pixel.

"Anyway, it seems Jenna is a hedge witch, whatever one of those is. But you know that, right?"

Actually, he didn't. Well, maybe when his brain was working right, he did. But right now, he could hardly even remember what she looked like. He *did* remember that she was his girlfriend, though, and that he really liked her. Well, maybe after a little rest, more of his mind would come back to him. He tried closing his eyes again, but the girl—Lahra, that's it, not Helaine!—shook him rather hard. He tried to tell her to stop it, but couldn't form the words properly.

"Stay awake!" Lahra ordered.

Well, he *would* stay awake—he just needed a little nap first . . . If only she'd stop shaking him, so he could get the rest he needed! But Lahra wouldn't. Despite his best efforts, she stopped him from sleeping. Dirty tricks, like pinching him, or trying to tickle him. Not fair!

Then Jenna was back. "Munson will be fine," she told Lahra. "He's just resting."

That's not fair! Pixel tried to protest. *You'll let him rest, why not me?* But his words just tumbled out, not making any sense. Maybe his brain was permanently injured, and he'd be a drooling idiot like this for the rest of his life? Pixel would rather be dead than damaged like that. Okay, if falling asleep might kill him—well, better that than an idiot . . .

Jenna held his hand and that felt nice. "I've done as much as I can with my gem," she told him. "We're really lucky the pirates didn't search us and take them from us. But the islanders don't have anything worth stealing, so I guess the raiders figured we didn't, either. If I only had my powders and potions!" She sounded terribly unhappy, and Pixel wished he could cheer her up. But he couldn't even speak properly.

Just a quick bit of shut-eye . . .

"Pixel!" Jenna yelled. "Stay awake! Focus on me! Think nice thoughts, something to make you happy, make you want to be well."

I do want to be well, Pixel tried to communicate. He knew it wasn't working, though. *I don't want to make you unhappy by dying, but I'm not sure I have much choice in the matter.* Well, maybe she could understand that without hearing him say it. He wished he could tell her goodbye before he died, but his mind and mouth didn't seem to be on speaking terms.

That was funny! He tried giggling, but the result was more like a convulsion. It worried Jenna more, so he tried to stop, but couldn't. Eventually, though, he was too tired to continue, and simply collapsed back again.

Lahra moved back to join them. "How is he?" she asked.

Jenna shook her head. "Very weak. He seems to be having fits or something." She bit at her lip. "There's only one thing I can think of doing now, and I'm not even sure it will work. I'm still rather new at this magic business." She took her aquamarine from its pouch. "This gives me the power of survival—in situations that might kill me, it gives me extra strength." She hesitated.

"What are you going to do?" Lahra asked. There was concern in her voice. Pixel wondered the same thing, but he didn't have to ability to ask.

"I'm going to transfer some of my own life energy into Pixel," Jenna said softly. "It should boost his strength. And the aquamarine should ensure that I don't kill myself doing it."

"Should?" Lahra echoed. "But you don't know?"

"I'll soon find out," Jenna answered. Pixel wanted to yell at her, to tell her it was too dangerous, and that he'd be fine. He just needed a bit of rest, that was all. But he couldn't speak, and could barely even blink his eyes. He was terribly afraid that Jenna would seriously injure herself with this untried magic. But he couldn't stop her. He couldn't stop a snail the shape he was in.

Jenna seized her gemstone and focused on it. She whispered words that Pixel couldn't make out, and then he could feel the tang of magic in the air. It was gathering about her, making her hair flicker and move. She had never looked prettier, and he hoped this wouldn't be his last memory of her. She reached out gently to touch him over the heart.

Then the power began to flow. She was channeling it, sending it flowing into his weak and dying body. He could feel the strength moving through his sinews, his muscles, his organs. His bones seemed stronger, his blood pounded harder, and the fog in his mind began to lift.

It was working!

But at what cost to Jenna? He could see that she was tiring swiftly, as her life-force flowed across to him. The aquamarine glowed blue and rich in her hand as she clutched it. But she seemed to be almost collapsing in upon herself. Even as Pixel could feel his life returning, Jenna seemed to be flickering and diminishing. Her hand felt cold on his chest.

He managed to gather the strength to reach out and touch her hand, and then he pushed at it, breaking their connection. Instantly, she fell back, completely exhausted, the light in the gem dying. Pixel could focus his mind now, but his body was still dangerously weak. He couldn't even move to check on her. Instead, he looked at Lahra and croaked, "Is she alive?"

Lahra bent to check, feeling for a pulse. "A little weak," she finally decided. "But she's alive. Do you think she'll recover?"

"She will, if I have anything to do with it," Pixel vowed. "She saved my life, and I'll make certain she doesn't pay for it with her own." He didn't know what he could do, though—but he was determined, and he wouldn't allow her to die.

If he had any say in the matter.

"I just need rest," he told Lahra. "Is there any water?" She nodded and ran to fetch some from a bucket. He sipped it from the ladle she brought, and then fell backward. "I'll be fine soon," he lied. "Just a little rest."

Lahra looked worried. "Jenna said you weren't to sleep."

"I won't," he promised. "I'm just conserving my strength. You go and see to your friend. I'll be fine." Lahra looked uncertain, but finally nodded and went off to check on Munson. Pixel propped himself against the wall behind him, and tried to see what resources of strength he now had.

Then he heard the sound of voices from above. Of course—it had to be the pirates, up on deck! He couldn't make out what they were saying, but they certainly sounded excited—and scared. There was some screaming, and the thunder of footsteps.

What could it be? Pixel grinned to himself. He could think of only one possibility—Score and Helaine had managed to catch up with the ship, and were storming it to free Jenna and himself! He could almost picture Helaine furiously hacking her way through any number of pirates—she would never allow anything to stop her. And Score would be doing something silly, as he always did. Good old Score!

There was a sudden flash of daylight in the hold, almost blinding him. The hatch above had been thrown open. It must mean rescue! Then a rope ladder was dropped down. But instead of Score and Helaine, two pirates swarmed down it.

"Pick one of the ones in worst shape," the captain called from above.

The two men glanced around the hold. Pixel could see that there were about thirty of the Harvesters in here, most cringing in fear against the opposite bulkhead. Lahra was with an injured man in the center of the room, and then he and Jenna were together. The pirates came over to them.

"What are you doing?" Pixel asked anxiously, struggling to get to his feet. But he still lacked the strength and coordination.

"He'll do," one of the men decided, and both of them grabbed him roughly, dragging him back to the ladder. A rope was tossed down, and tied under his arms. He was hauled up, spinning as he went. The dizziness did nothing to help his state of mind.

When he was on the deck, other hands grabbed him, and pulled the rope free. Then he was carried to the side of the ship. It was hard for him to make anything out, as he was carried face down, but he felt the hands holding him suddenly start swinging him back and forth.

"Over the side with him, lads!" the captain yelled. "If it has something to eat, maybe that beast will leave us alone!"

What? Before Pixel could react, he felt himself flying through the air, and then there was a tremendous blow on his back as he hit the water. He sank beneath the waves for a second, and then bobbed up, choking and spluttering, hacking water from his lungs.

Then his head cleared a little. Maybe the shock of the frigid water had helped, but he could begin thinking clearly again. And at what a time! He could see that he was being swept away from the ship, which had piled sail on and was running with the wind as fast as it was able.

Then he saw the thing it was running from. It looked like a dinosaur, or maybe a dragon—all long neck, teeth, and spines. It was huge, and it was clearly looking for a meal.

And he was it. The beast had seen him, and was cutting through the water toward him. Pixel had a moment of blind panic before he found himself clutching one of his gemstones. It was his topaz, for controlling fire.

Fire? Out here in the ocean?

Yes! His mind was working again. Fire was simply heat in any form, and all matter possessed it. All he had to do was to control the heat flow . . . Instead of *sending* fire, he would *withdraw* it . . . He concentrated as much as he was able, and then set the magic to work.

When heat is taken from it, water freezes . . .

The sea monster roared in shock and terror as ice began to form all around it. Pixel concentrated, drawing the heat from the water and radiating it away. The water froze, and in moments the startled sea monster was half-encased in ice.

He was safe from it now. The ice would melt in a couple of hours, freeing the monster. But they should be far, far apart by that time, and he'd be safe.

He glanced around, and was shocked. There was no sign of the ship. While he'd been casting his spell, it had gone. He had no idea in which direction—he was all turned around by the action of the waves—so he didn't even have a clue where to start looking.

Worse than that—he was a very poor swimmer, and he'd used almost all of his remaining strength for that spell. Plus, his clothes were getting water-logged, and were heavy. He could feel all of this acting together on him, dragging him down.

The next time his head went under the water, he didn't have the strength to push it out again. He was holding his breath, but he couldn't manage that for very long.

He was going to drown in moments . . .

8

Jenna was too weak to do anything to prevent Pixel being taken. She could tell her own life was hanging on by only the thinnest of magical threads. The aquamarine was sustaining her, and rebuilding her strength, but it might take hours. And it would take longer than that before she could use her magic again. All she could do was panic—why did they want Pixel? Clearly for no good reason . . .

Lahra crept to a slight gap in the wall, and peered through. Jenna could feel the tension in her as she watched. "What is it?" she asked.

Lahra stared at her. "They . . . they threw him overboard," she gasped. "And there's a Devourer out there—it eats *anything* . . . Oh, Jenna, I'm so sorry!"

Jenna was stunned. Pixel—*gone?* Could it be possible? Sweet, kind-hearted, impractical Pixel? Dead? Her heart felt as if it had turned to ice, freezing her entire body. Poor, poor, Pixel!

"No!" she decided. "No! I won't believe it! I *won't!* He's too inventive to die like that. I *won't* believe it."

Lahra came to her and held her tight. "Denial," she said. "I know, you can't bring yourself to believe it. But you'll have to face it, Jenna—he's gone. Even if he's somehow survived the Devourer—and nobody ever has—then he'll be lost at sea, and drown, no matter how good a swimmer he is."

"He's a terrible swimmer," Jenna gasped. "He told me so. He's kind of helpless in many ways, and really strong in others. But he'll think of some way out of it, I know he will."

Was she just fooling herself? But it hurt so much to think that Pixel could be dead. It was as if someone had ripped out some vital organ. She felt as if she, too, were dying.

"Jenna, he was almost dead when they tossed him overboard," Lahra said sadly. "It doesn't matter how inventive he is, the odds are too great against him."

"He'll beat them." Jenna wasn't sure whether that was just wishful thinking or real certainty, but at the moment she'd take either. She *had* to believe that Pixel was somehow still alive, otherwise, she'd just collapse in pain and tears.

"But I can't afford to be distracted by mourning him—even if I should be. One of us may be next." That thought had clearly not occurred to Lahra. She went pale, and huddled closer to Jenna, this time for comfort for herself.

Jenna couldn't help feeling sorry for these Harvesters. They were used to a calm, peaceful life, with no aggression. They simply lived quietly, growing and harvesting their crops and raising their families. She had almost envied them—they didn't know the pain of working for any nobles, as her people did. They never suffered the agonies of war being forced upon them. It was almost a paradise for them—way too dull for her, but she imagined that they were used to it.

And now their entire world had been turned upside down. Violence, brutal attacks, and slavery had intruded on their idyll, and they were not at all able to cope with it. Even the thought of fighting back was alien to them. They were like children, lost and in need of an adult to guide them.

Which left her as their protector. If Pixel was dead—and he *wasn't*!—then she knew what he would want of her. He would wish her to look after these helpless folk, and protect them, even at the cost of her own life. Jenna didn't have a clue yet as to how she could even begin to manage that, but she knew she would have to do it—Pixel would expect it of her. And her own upbringing had been to aid the sick and helpless, so she couldn't turn her back on them now.

If only Score were here! He was sarcastic and silly, but he had a good heart—and even though he claimed to be a coward, he was the second bravest boy she knew, after Pixel. And even Helaine—she might be an icy, arrogant, spoiled brat, but there was no doubting her courage and determination. She would take on all of these pirates without hesitation. Jenna realized that there were certain times when even a noble might be useful.

And, to be honest, Helaine was not as bad as most. She did sometimes, at least, try to be pleasant. Not often, maybe, and not very much, but the fact that she tried at all was to her credit. Hanging around Score and Pixel seemed to be doing her good. Maybe she'd even unbend sufficiently one day to become human . . .

But neither were here—she was alone, and the only defense that these people had. She was certain that the pirates had nothing good in store for them, so it was up to her to do what she could. It might be too little, and she might die in trying—but she was absolutely determined to give it her best shot.

But she could do nothing while she was weak and helpless like this. She needed to gather her strength. And that meant rest.

"Lahra," she said. "I have to sleep. I'm useless like this. Wake me if anything at all happens, okay?" Lahra nodded her promise, and Jenna let her mind go free.

Her last thought before sleep took her was of Pixel . . .

Jenna struggled back awake, realizing her shoulders were being shaken. She opened her eyes. "What?" she gasped.

"We've arrived—wherever we were heading," Lahra whispered. "The pirates have tied the ship up. It feels—strange."

Jenna nodded, and took an inventory. She was still weak, but a lot stronger than she had been. At least half-restored, she knew. She could do with more rest, and food, but doubted she'd get much of either. Now that they had arrived at their destination, she expected that things would start happening. She had to bury her fears about Pixel, knowing they would tear her apart if she didn't.

With a rumble, the hatchway to the hold was thrown back, and light streamed in again. The prisoners all shaded their eyes. Shapes of men appeared about the hole, and the rope ladder snaked down.

"Climb out, scum!" one of the men called. "Anyone who doesn't, or can't, we kill. Move!"

Terrified and helpless, the Harvesters began to do as they were told. As they reached the deck, rough hands grabbed them and threw them aside to make room for the next prisoner. Jenna staggered to her feet, gratefully accepting help from Lahra. Together they moved toward the ladder. Then Jenna shrugged off Lahra's hand. "Your friend, Munson," she said, pointing to where the man lay in the corner. "He needs your help more. I'll be fine," she lied.

Lahra looked concerned, but then nodded and rushed to help Munson. Jenna focused on moving her feet until she reached the ladder. It took her two attempts to grip the first rung, and then she climbed, slowly and painfully. Finally, she reached the deck, only to be halted by a sword point in her face.

"She's not strong enough to work," the pirate wielding it decided. "I'll just kill her now." Jenna braced for the death thrust, knowing she had no reserves of strength or magic with which to fight it.

"No," the captain said, shoving the blade aside. "If she got this far, she can at least do some work. Let *that* kill her." He gestured, and Jenna was dragged from the ladder and flung to the deck with the other prisoners. She was too exhausted to be grateful she'd been spared. She didn't even try to get up, just lay there for a moment.

Munson wasn't as lucky. Lahra seemed to have managed to get him to the ladder, but there was no way she could get him up it. His shoulder had been badly inflamed, Jenna knew, and without her poultices and potions, she'd been unable to bring the swelling down.

The pirate captain, in disgust, snatched a crossbow from one of his men and fired it.

"You, girl," he yelled into the hold. "Leave that carcass and get up here, or the next bolt is for you!" Sobbing, Lahra climbed out of the hold and rushed to Jenna.

"They murdered him!" she gasped. "He couldn't climb, so they killed him!"

"They will pay," Jenna vowed. "All of them. They have much to pay for."

"We can do nothing," Lahra sobbed.

"Yet," Jenna corrected her. If she could only get through the rest of this terrible day, a good night's sleep, and some food would work wonders for her. Then let the pirates beware! She didn't know what she would do, but she would do *something*!

"All right," Black Hawk snarled. "Over the side with you. If there's any trouble from you at all, you'll be beaten. And if there's more trouble, you'll be killed. I trust I make myself clear?" He looked at them all, and laughed. "Yes, I see from the fear in your eyes that I do. Well, remember this lesson, and you may live—for a while. Now—ashore!"

Jenna found the strength to clamber to her feet. Lahra held her arm, but Jenna wasn't sure who was supporting whom. The islander was shaking, obviously terrified and in emotional turmoil. Jenna willed the other girl to hold up, knowing full well how difficult it was when your entire world view was turned upside down. It wasn't that long ago that Jenna had experienced much the same thing.

The difference between them was that Jenna had been made stronger by it. And now was the time for this strength to hold them both up.

The ship had docked at an island. Jenna heard Lahra gasp, and couldn't understand why for a moment. Then she realized that this was the first time in her life that the Harvester had ever seen solid land.

"It's unnatural," the girl gasped. "These people must be sicker than I ever imagined."

Jenna almost smiled. Now wasn't the time to tell Lahra that she herself lived on dry land. "Bear up," she murmured.

"No talking!" Black Hawk ordered. "You're here to exercise your muscles, not your tongues!"

There was a plank connecting the ship to a wooden structure on the island. Jenna had to concentrate—Score had told her what this sort of thing was before they had left on their—ha! vacation . . . A jetty, that was it. The pirates pushed the startled and

113

scared islanders onto the plank leading from the ship to the jetty. The islanders hesitated to leave the familiar feel of the sea for the unknown, but they were prodded on by weapons. Jenna gripped Lahra's arm as firmly as she could, and the two of them walked down the plank. It bent beneath them under their weight, which gave Jenna a bad moment or two. Then they were on the wooden jetty.

Startlingly, it felt really odd. Jenna's body had become used to the swaying of the sea, and now she was suddenly back on dry land again, it felt as if it was the land that was swaying beneath her feet. It was much worse for Lahra and the other islanders, of course. The land had *never* been firm beneath them, and the experience was terrifying. All of them stumbled as they came ashore, and several of them actually fell. Lahra would have done so, had Jenna not managed to find the strength to support her. "It will get better," Jenna promised the moaning girl.

The pirates were laughing at the discomfort of their captives, and actually gave them a moment's breather while they amused themselves seeing the islanders stumble and panic. Rage boiled up inside of Jenna; these people were truly evil, and needed to be punished. She could not accomplish this yet—but she would. She would make Pixel proud of her, whether he was alive or . . .

No! She wasn't even going to *think* that!

While the pirates laughed, she glanced around. There was a second ship already there, similar to the one they had arrived on, but manned by only a handful of pirates. They, too, watched in amusement.

Eventually, the pirates' entertainment dried up, and they started to prod the captives forward with their swords. They all stumbled drunkenly from the jetty to dry land.

Jenna couldn't see how large the island was. There was a beach stretching to the left, and solid land to the right, both at least a mile long. Ahead of them, she could see that the island rose to a flattened peak. Smoke was issuing from this. She remembered from lessons she'd shared with Pixel that this meant the mountain was actually a volcano. He had told her about strange places where mountains rumbled, and from which came melted rocks like rivers. It had been hard to believe, but she knew that Pixel wouldn't lie to her.

Pixel! Poor, poor Pixel . . . Jenna fought back tears. She would be strong. She would be!

There was a path of sorts leading from the dock up the slope of the volcano. It was hard to see where it might go. There weren't any tall trees here, as there were on her home world of Ordin, or on her adopted world of Dondar. It was all shrubbery and trees that were scraggly and ill-looking. But they were enough to cover the slopes, and hide the pathway from view.

"Move!" one of the pirates yelled. The terrified islanders lurched on their way, driven by blows and laughter. Jenna hunched down and grimly forced herself to move on. She still desperately needed rest, and her stomach growled, reminding her that it had been—well, she didn't know *how* long since she had last eaten. And her lips and throat were dry. She couldn't imagine that the pirates would bother to let them rest, or feed them yet, so she tried to ignore her pangs.

The pathway led away from the ocean, and that terrified the captives further. Each step they took away from the only life they had ever known was into probable pain and certain fear. Some of the pirates had whips, though, and Jenna heard them crack out, followed by cries of pain.

"On, you dogs!"

There was no choice. The prisoners moved on, farther from their beloved, safe sea, and deeper into the unknown.

Jenna studied as much as she could on their journey. Pixel had always said that knowledge was power, so she needed as much as she could gather. She fought down her feelings as she realized just how much of her life was now filled by him, even when he wasn't here. Even when he might never be here again . . . She would weep later, she promised herself. Now she had to be strong, not only for herself, but for her companions. The pathway, focus on the pathway! She realized that it was fairly new—only a few months old, not ancient, such as paths were on Ordin. So the pirates had not been here for very long. Also, there were no signs of any other construction, save for the jetty. Well, there wasn't any wood really to build anything. The ships must have been constructed elsewhere, and the wood for the jetty must have been brought here, unless the rest of the island was very different from this portion.

So whatever the pirates were up to was probably recently started. It was most puzzling. Pixel might be able to make sense from all of this, but she couldn't.

Eventually, about twenty minutes later, the path started to get more rugged. Rock walls rose on either side of the pathway, and they were in a small valley of sorts. Jenna saw that it led into a large cave ahead of them. There were more pirates there, clearly on guard duty. Jenna suspected that this meant that there were more slaves here, and that guess turned out to be accurate. They were led into the cave, which was about ten feet tall at the entrance. It expanded inside, branching in several directions. It was gloomy, but not dark.

Jenna had expected to see torches burning, but there weren't any. It took her a moment to understand why, and then it made sense—there wasn't enough wood here on this island to waste it by burning it. Instead, there was some sort of moss on the walls that glowed faintly, sufficiently to dimly illuminate the cave. The captives were herded to the left. There was a second, smaller cave, where wooden posts were erected to serve as a jail. Inside the cave were probably two or three dozen other captives, all scared and silent.

One of the pirates unfastened a small door, and the new arrivals were forced inside the prison. The pirate captain and a few men entered behind them. Jenna and Lahra huddled together for comfort.

Black Hawk stood in front of them, arms on hips, grinning nastily. "You scum won't be fit to work until the morning," he told them contemptuously. "You'll be used to the feel of dry land beneath your feet by them. You'll be fed and given water today out of the kindness of our hearts." The pirates behind him all laughed at this ridiculous claim. "But, starting tomorrow, you'll work. And if you don't work, you don't eat or drink. And if you don't work hard enough, we'll kill you." He glared around. "Are there any questions?"

One of the islanders—a tall, skinny man—shuffled his feet. "What is it that you want us to do?"

"A good question," Black Hawk said. "We want you to dig." He nodded, and one of his men stepped forward. He raised a whip, and lashed out. The islander who'd asked the question screamed, and fell to the ground. "Now, are there any further questions?" He looked around, and seemed pleased at the silence. "Good. You fools are starting to learn. You might actually survive this—for a while." He turned his back contemptuously, and he and his men left the cell. The door was closed and fastened behind him.

The other prisoners started to moan and shake with fear. Jenna moved forward, toward the whipped man.

She had little healing magic, but she would do what she could for the poor victim. Grimly, she realized that whatever help she gave him would only prolong his suffering.

There didn't seem to be any way out of this hell hole except by dying . . .

9

Score was feeling rather pleased with himself. His idea of using a seashell and expanding it into a kind of boat had worked perfectly. He and Helaine had been able to alternate using their magic to move it, and none of the local sea monsters had even attempted to bother them. Their guide, Larmon, was the quiet type, who seemed happy enough to sit quietly, watching their way, and only calling out the occasional course adjustment.

But Helaine was brooding. Score couldn't quite understand why—okay, so Pixel and Jenna were most likely in trouble—but it wasn't like *that* was anything new. They were both powerful—even on this Rim World—and skilled, so Score was pretty certain they'd be fine when he and Helaine caught up with them. Then the four of them together should be able to whup anything they came across. End of problem, surely?

"I'd offer you a penny for your thoughts," Score said to her. "Except I think that's overvaluing them."

Helaine blinked at him in confusion. Right, no pennies on her world, so the insult had gone right over her head. "I have a bad feeling," she told him.

"It's most likely that squid they gave us for lunch," Score answered. "I'm not sure it was quite dead, and I'm not a sushi fanatic."

"The food was adequate," Helaine replied. "That's not what I was referring to."

"I didn't really think it was," Score said. "Jeez, I really wish that you'd grow a sense of humor one of these days. You really need to lighten up some."

"And you need to develop a sense of responsibility and to know when levity is appropriate," Helaine countered. "So we are even." She shook her head. "I can feel trouble."

"Yeah, you're good at that," Score agreed. It was her special gift, and very helpful for a warrior. He scanned the sea, and there was nothing in sight except . . . well, sea. Lots of it. "Imminent danger, or just danger hanging around in the background?"

"I do not know," Helaine confessed. "It's a sort of permanent thing."

"That's our life," Score complained. "Permanent danger." Then he grinned. "And a few laughs."

"No, not that sort of thing." Helaine shook her head. "I can't really explain it, I'm afraid. There's something out there after us, but I can't get more specific. It's the kind of feeling I had when the Shadows were hunting us. I *know* it's there, but not in any one place or at any one time. Just threatening. It makes me uneasy."

Score didn't like the way her brooding was going. Okay, so there was danger—what else was new? But he needed Helaine sharp, her skills ready, not in this introspective, depressed state.

"There's a ship ahead," Larmon said in his quiet way. "There."

He was quite correct—it was barely more than a speck, but it was obviously a ship. "We're catching up with them," he said happily.

123

"Not necessarily the one with Pixel and Jenna aboard," Helaine pointed out. "Our pirate prisoner told us that there are three pirate ships. Besides, it might be just some more islanders."

"Not islanders," Larmon insisted. "That's too big a ship for us. It's the pirates all right."

"Good," Score said. "And I don't much care which ship it is—there's almost certainly prisoners aboard who need rescuing." Helaine was using her magic at the moment to propel their sea shellcraft. "Helaine, I'd better take over moving this thing—you save your strength. You're going to need it to attack."

Larmon looked worried. "Three of us against a ship-ful of pirates?" he questioned, looking very worried.

"*Two* of us," Helaine corrected. "After all, we want to give them a fair fight."

Score raised an eyebrow. "Hey, that was a joke. Not a very good one, but definitely the right species. You're starting to live right, my girl." He patted her shoulder. "I'm very proud of you."

"Concentrate on moving our craft," she told him with a sigh. But he was sure there was a little sparkle in her eye. Maybe she actually did like him—or maybe it was just the anticipation she felt for a good fight.

They were catching up quite quickly with the ship now, and it was growing steadily larger. Larmon gave a grunt. "Not the one that attacked us," he said.

"How can you be sure?" Score asked.

"Broader in the beam. It's also lower in the water, so I'd say there are more slaves aboard."

Score couldn't tell the difference, but Larmon was the expert, so he accepted his opinion. "Right, let's get ready to kick butt." He was a little tired from propelling their shell, but he still had sufficient strength in reserve for a quick fight. He hoped it would be a quick fight. "Battle plan?" he asked Helaine.

"Simple," she replied. "You and I get aboard and take out the pirates. Larmon, you follow, and set the prisoners free. See if they can help in the fight."

Score nodded. "Yeah, that's simple. Now, we just hope that the pirates know that their part is to lose the battle." He started to form up a large fireball. The rigging and sails looked like they'd burn really nicely, and it would bring the ship to a halt.

"What are you doing?" Helaine asked, alarmed. "You can't burn the ship!"

"Why not?" Score asked. "You thinking of offering them a good trade-in deal for a new model?"

"If you burn the ship," Helaine said patiently, "then what will we use to get the prisoners home again in?"

"Oh." She had a good point there. "Okay, no destroying the ship, then." He stared at the fireball he'd conjured up. "But I hate to let a good ball of fire go to waste . . . so . . ." He threw it high into the air, and then exploded it over the ship.

The pirates clearly hadn't seen their tiny vessel, and the explosion startled them all. They swarmed on deck and into the rigging to try and see what was going on.

"Wonderful," Helaine sighed. "You just ruined the element of surprise."

"Yeah, but I scared the heck out of them. They're going to be really demoralized when we attack them."

"I *really* have to teach you tactics one day," Helaine muttered. By now, they were close to the side of the ship. There were several pirates getting ready to fire crossbows at them. Score used his power to change the crossbow bolts into glue. They not only gummed up the bows, but stuck the pirates to their weapons.

Helaine levitated herself up to the deck of the ship. Seeing a girl flying certainly scared the pirates even more. They might know about magic, but it was clearly something that they didn't see too often. Helaine's captured sword was in her hands, and she advanced on the closest knot of men.

Score was stuck using the more conventional approach—climbing up one of the ropes that hung over the side. Larmon was right behind him—the Harvester might not be a fighter, but he was clearly not a coward, either.

"Surrender now," Helaine suggested. "It will save you a great deal of pain if you do."

"It's just a girl and a couple of weak boys," one of the pirates growled. "We can take them." He rushed at Helaine, waving his own sword.

"Famous last words," Score said with a grin.

Helaine parried the attacker's first clumsy blow, spun, and used her own sword to slash at his arm. The man screamed, and dropped his weapon, bleeding badly. "First blood to the *girl*," she said. She kicked him in the small of his back, and sent him stumbling to the deck, turning to face the other pirates. "Who's next?"

They weren't stupid. Three of them rushed her at once. Helaine gave a wild laugh and leaped to meet them, swords clanging and drawing sparks as they met.

"You wouldn't know she was a magic user," Score muttered to himself. "She just likes beating people up . . ." He himself preferred to stay far, far away from anyone he was fighting—much less risk that way. Clutching his emerald, he started in with his usual fighting tricks. He turned the air his foes breathed into laughing gas. Several of them started to giggle and then collapsed, sleeping blissfully. This startled their companions, who couldn't see any reason for their falls. While they hesitated to attack this strange foe, Score started flinging mud, glue, and custard pies at them. Under this bizarre barrage, the pirates started to fall back. They weren't really very used to fighting on this world—just holding a sword or a crossbow meant they could take charge of the peaceful Harvesters simply enough. Nobody had ever really fought back against them. Now they were facing a magic user and a girl with skills that were far greater than their own.

Score took a quick glance over at Helaine. He wasn't actually worried about her, but he did like to make sure she was okay from time to time. Grinning, he saw that she'd flattened three pirates already, and had two more backed against the railings. Both of them were sweating and looking quite frightened.

Larmon had vanished, and Score hoped he was doing his job and freeing the Harvesters. Satisfied things were going well, Score scanned the ship's deck. Aside from the two scared pirates Helaine was beating, there were just four more left. These men, seeing the havoc on the deck of the ship, seemed to be uncertain what they should do. All of them were young and nervous.

Score grinned, and conjured up another fireball, which he held in the palm of his hand. Seeing it hovering there, not burning him, seemed to scare the pirates even more. "Right," Score told them. "You've got a choice now—you can surrender peacefully, or else I'll lob this at you and you can burn horribly to death. Which will it be?"

As one, the four men dropped their swords and fell to their knees.

"Smart boys," Score said, approvingly. He made the fireball fade away. "Okay, maybe you'd better start tying each other up—I can never remember a reef knot from a sheep-shank."

Suddenly, something hit him in the back, knocking him to the deck, stunned. He barely had a second to roll over onto his back before a long, curved sword slammed into the deck where his head had been. He didn't even have the time to be scared as his attacker raised the weapon to strike again. The man was dressed elaborately, with a flashing jewel on a chain around his neck. Score guessed that this was the captain, and that he was *really* unhappy at what had happened to his ship. The sword whistled down, aimed to slice Score's neck in half. He couldn't think of anything in his final second that might stop the blow.

Then there was the sound of metal on metal, and Helaine's throaty laugh. "Not fair, attacking a man without a sword," she cried, forcing the captain back. "Try me instead."

Score almost fainted from relief as Helaine slammed blow after blow at the pirate, sending him back, step by step. The man was clearly outclassed, and knew it. Helaine's blade flickered out, slicing through the captain's sleeve, and leaving a long line of crimson. A second blow left a red scar under his left eye.

"Enough!" he cried, and dropped his weapon. "I surrender!" Helaine looked rather disappointed.

Score scrambled to his feet again. "Hey, what do you know?" he called. "We've captured ourselves a genuine pirate ship!"

10

Helaine grinned at Score's enthusiasm. "And now that we've captured it, what do we do?" She was fine in battles, but the more complex plans were up to Pixel, or, in a pinch, Score. She knew that she tended to be very blunt in her solutions to problems, and that sometimes a bit more subtlety was called for.

Larmon had freed the captives, who were stumbling on deck, blinking in the bright light of the sun. Score gestured at them.

"Well, we have our own crew now, so I think it's time these pirates got a taste of their own medicine." He turned to Larmon. "Alright, you're appointed first mate. As soon as your friends are feeling better, bundle the pirates into the hold and lock them in. I assume these Harvesters can sail this ship?"

Larmon shrugged. "It's bigger than the ones we're used to, but it shouldn't be too difficult. Where do you want to head?"

"For the island," Score said. "There's still two more ship loads of captives to be freed."

One of the ex-captives looked startled. "We're not fighters! Now that we have a ship, we should just go home."

Helaine was disgusted with him. "What? Now that *we* risked our lives to save you, you want to turn tail and run, and leave others as captives? What kind of people are you?"

"The lass is right," one of the women captives said. "We can't run away. We have to help."

"But we're not fighters," the man insisted. "What can we do?"

"What we can't," Score said firmly. "Sail. We need a crew, and you're it. When we get to the island, Helaine and I will fight. You guys just stay with the ship, and any others we can capture. I'm sure you can manage that."

"There will be more pirates there," the man objected.

"Parffy, you were always a weakling," the woman sneered. "I think I speak for the rest of us when I say we'll help as we can. Right?" The other islanders didn't sound as certain, but Helaine was relieved when they sided with the woman. They did need help, even if it wasn't skilled.

"Right." Score grinned again, and turned back to Larmon. "Okay, first mate, you get this ship underway for the island again. How long will it take, do you think?"

Larmon studied the sky and the sea. "Probably not long—by morning, I'd say. I need the night for the stars, so I can be certain where we are."

"Morning." Score shook his head. "I hate leaving our friends captives that long. But if there's no other way . . . Okay, let's see about getting our crew into action, eh?"

Helaine watched with some amusement as Score and Larmon managed to get the islanders working. In a short while, the pirates were all imprisoned below, and the ship sailed on. Score moved up onto the captain's deck, and Larmon took the helm.

"You're enjoying this, aren't you?" she asked Score.

"Hey, every kid likes to play pirates," he replied. "Maybe even you. This is fun—if you forget that Pix and Jenna are still captives." He snapped his fingers. "Hey, I should have thought of it before—can't you contact them using your agate?"

Helaine shook her head. "I've tried, but we seem to be too far apart. Maybe in the morning, when we're closer to the island. On this Rim World, my magic just isn't strong enough."

"You're doing fine," Score assured her. "We'll just have to improvise, as always."

Helaine snorted. "Yes, that does seem to be our style." Then she scowled. "Hey, you're the captain, and Larmon's the first mate. What am I?"

"The boarding party," Score answered. "When it comes to fighting, there's nobody I'd sooner have in charge."

Helaine nodded happily. Score had certainly changed since she'd first met him—back then he'd hated the fact that she was a girl and could outfight him. Now he simply accepted it as a fact, and had come to rely upon her skills. And she knew she'd changed, too—she thought he was weak and foolish when they'd first teamed up. Now she understood that a lot of his foolishness was a mask to hide his real feelings. And the fact that he wasn't a warrior didn't bother her at all—he fought well in many other ways.

In fact, when it came time to marry, she knew she could do a lot worse than him. Especially if he was, as it appeared, the heir to the throne of Ordin. Her father certainly approved of the match. But Score wasn't as keen on starting up a relationship as Pixel. He was used to being a loner, and still had trouble acting as part of a team sometimes. Still, it was nice to know that he relied on her—as she knew she could on him. For all of his talk of cowardice, he rarely backed down when he was helping others.

Night fell quickly, and the women on the ship cooked up a nice meal. Helaine's stomach reminded her how long it had been since she had last eaten, so the meal was doubly welcome.

"Fish again," Score complained. "What I'd give right now for a good hamburger, or slice of pizza." He munched on the filet.

"You could always use your power to change it if you wanted," Helaine pointed out.

"Waste of my strength," Score told her. Helaine wasn't fooled for a minute—the meal was good; Score just liked to complain.

"Save your strength," she agreed. "We're going to have a busy day tomorrow. These pirates must be smashed. They hurt too many people."

"Yeah." Score was quiet for a moment. "The thing that bothers me is what we're going to do with them. I mean, we can't kill them. And it's not practical to keep them captives forever. And I don't think I'd trust any of them if they claimed that they wanted to go straight."

"You'll think of something," Helaine said. "I have confidence in you. Or Pixel will have a solution when we find him. He always has ideas."

"That's true." Score grinned. "I'll let it be his problem." He turned to Larmon, who was still at the helm. "So, how's the navigating going?"

"We were not far out," the man answered. "I've corrected our course. We'll reach the island very early in the morning. Then what?"

"Well, then we dock," Score said. "They're expecting another ship, aren't they?" He looked at his clothing. "But I think we'd all better get some more flashy pirate garb. We should be able to fool them into thinking we're their friends . . ."

As morning dawned, Helaine wriggled uncomfortably in her borrowed clothing. She wore pants, boots, and a very frilly shirt. She had managed to convince Score that she *really* didn't need an eye patch as well. But he'd insisted on her wearing a wide-brimmed hat, with her hair tucked up inside it. "There are no pirate wenches in this crew," he'd pointed out. "So you'd better look like Renald again." To be honest, she quite liked the hat, so she didn't complain too badly.

Score was dressed just as flashily, and he'd made the islanders dress in the same fashion. As the ship drew closer to the island, Helaine had to admit that they did look the part of desperate pirates.

The island wasn't very large—perhaps five or six miles across, and vaguely half-moon shaped. The center of the island was a large volcano, and smoke rose from it that could be seen a long way off at sea. It was such a relief to see solid land again after so long with nothing but sea around them. As they approached, she could make out a dock, and two other ships tied up.

"Right," Score said. "Helaine and I will do the fighting. I should think there will be only a skeleton crew on each of the other ships. When we take the pirates, you guys scuttle those ships. Burn them to the water, if you can. This one should have plenty of room to take everyone home." Larmon and his friends nodded. They looked quite relieved that they wouldn't be needed in the fighting. Score turned to Helaine. "Okay, boarding party? All set?"

She held up her sword. "I am ready."

"Well, don't get carried away with hacking everyone into tiny bits," Score reminded her. "Remember, you can do magic, and it's not dishonorable to use it on these scurvy dogs."

"What's a scurvy dog?" she asked.

"Come on, you dress like a pirate, start talking like one." Score grinned again. "Avast there, me hearties!" he yelled, as the ship slipped toward the dock. "Make ready to tie her up."

"It might be better if you let the sailors among us do this sort of work," Larmon suggested. Score flushed, and nodded. Helaine grinned at his discomfort.

"Do what you do best," she suggested.

"Yeah, but I can't run away on the water," he complained.

The other pirates on the two ships had spotted them by now, and were waving. Helaine saw that Score was correct—there was a minimal crew on each ship. She counted quickly—only ten men in all. The other pirates and their captives had to be elsewhere on the island. They'd have to question a captive later to discover where.

As Larmon and his helpers brought their ship in smoothly to the dock, and started throwing lines, Score nodded to Helaine. She understood. Clutching her sapphire in her left hand, she levitated herself and Score swiftly to the closer of the two other ships.

The watching pirates were startled. As before, it was clear that they were not used to seeing magic in operation. When they saw Helaine's raised sword, though, they understood enough to go for their own weapons.

Helaine plowed into the closest, slamming the hilt of her sword against his head before he could get his own weapon free. Stunned, he fell, out of the fight. The next two men had time to draw their weapons and meet her charge, though. But, despite their dress and manner, they were really only islanders who'd turned pirates. They weren't used to actually fighting anyone who fought back. She disarmed and wounded them both. Normally, she wouldn't have hurt a weaker foe, but these bullies deserved to suffer. The final two men on this ship were already out of action, covered in sticky glue, thanks to Score's magic.

"Didn't even work up a sweat," he said, cheerfully. "These guys are pushovers."

"Don't make the mistake of getting careless," Helaine warned him. "Even an incompetent foe can get in a lucky blow once in a while."

"Stop worrying, Mommy," Score mocked. "I'll be careful, and I always watch out when I fight big, bad pirates."

Helaine was annoyed with his flippant attitude. "You're asking to get hurt," she warned him. "If not by them, by me. Get ready." Then she flew the two of them to the final ship.

The pirates here had been warned by seeing what had happened to their companions on the other ship and, as she'd worried, were a bit more prepared. There had been six of them, but only four were now visible. Helaine wondered where the other two were—could they have run away, scared? Or were they up to something?

Her sense of danger warned her that something was wrong, and she dived to one side, pushing Score the other way as she moved. He yelped and fell, caught unaware by the action. A second later a weighted net fell over him from the rigging. He tried to get to his feet, but was swiftly entangled in its meshes.

Helaine might have cut him free with a couple of strokes from her blade, but she didn't get the chance; the other four pirates rushed her, their weapons waving wildly. Her only luck was that they tended to get in each other's way, but even she would have problems facing four swords at once.

Which meant it was time to take Score's advice and use magic instead. Her chrysoprase gave her control over the element of earth; this didn't simply mean soil, but anything connected with the earth. Since metals were dug from the earth, she could influence them. Reaching out with her power, she felt for the strength and solidity in the blades her opponents carried—and then took that strength from them. The pirates all gasped and drew to a halt when their swords all suddenly seemed to droop and melt. They wouldn't be able to fight anyone with floppy weapons! Grinning, Helaine launched herself at the men, and used the flat of her blade and the pommel to pummel them into submission or unconsciousness. Then she turned to see how Score was doing.

He'd been caught completely unawares by the net. Well, she'd warned him not to be so sure of himself— and he hadn't listened, which was par for his course. The two pirates who'd dropped the net onto him had jumped from the rigging and set about punching Score with wooden staves.

Even though he was trapped and howling from the beating he was getting, Score was still thinking. Helaine felt him reach out with his power of his chrysolite, and control water. He brought a large wave crashing over the deck, drenching his attackers and sweeping them off their feet. Then he turned the water into ice, freezing them in one place.

Helaine walked over to him as he struggled in the net, and cocked her head to one side. "Do you think you might start listening to me now?" she inquired.

"Yeah, yeah," he said, dismissively. "You going to cut me free or just lecture me?"

"Lecture you," she replied.

"Fine," he growled. "I'll do it myself." Using his power to transform things, he turned the ropes to water, and they dissolved about him. "You really like to say 'I told you so', don't you?"

"If you ever actually *listened* when I did, I'd stop," she informed him. "You are going to get yourself killed if you don't pay better attention in a fight. And when you do, don't come crying to me."

Score managed a weak grin. "Hey, *another* joke. Still feeble, but it is kind of funny. The next thing you know, you'll be making up limericks."

"I doubt it," she answered. She didn't even know what a limerick was, but she had no intention of letting him explain. "Well, despite your set back, the ships are ours, and the enemy captives. What do we do next?"

"Find somewhere to lock them away," he replied. "They must have some sort of jail around here where they keep their slaves. I'm sure that will do. Let's just get some information, shall we?" He walked to the two men he had frozen in ice. "Hey, guys, how's it going? You chilling in there?" Both were starting to look very cold.

"Filthy magic user!" one of the men said, attempting to spit. But he was shaking too much to manage it.

"I am *not* a filthy magic user!" Score protested. "I have a bath once a week, whether I need it or not." He sniffed. "Which is more than I can say for you. Okay, listen up—the two of you had better start answering my questions, or else."

"Or else what?" the second captive asked. He sounded frozen and frightened. Helaine smiled inwardly—this was the one who would crack for them.

She held up her sword. "Or else I'll start cutting you free. Of course, with all that ice, my blade is likely to slip . . ." She whirled, and brought her sword down close to the man's shoulder. She deliberately let it slide along the ice, nicking his exposed neck. Blood trickled down. "Oops."

"Don't!" he screamed. "What do you want to know?"

"There's a nice, cooperative piratesicle," Score said approvingly. "I'll keep my homicidal friend here away from you as long as you talk. So, first question, for one hundred dollars—where are the prisoners?"

"In the mine!" the man said, quickly. "They're working in the mine!"

"Hey, good," Score told him, patting his head. "Hey, that cut isn't *too* deep, is it? Looks like it's bleeding quite a bit. Oh, well, once we're done here, I'll have it seen to. Right, next question—where's the mine?"

"Up the path," the man babbled. "There's a cave at the end. The mine's below that."

"Okay, bonus round—is there somewhere there where we can keep you and your buddies imprisoned while we go take out the rest of your slimy friends?"

"There's a cell in the cave, where the prisoners are kept before they go down into the mines," the man gasped.

Score scowled. "And when they come back?"

The man tried shaking his head, and then panicked as he saw blood flying from the wound on his neck. He couldn't see the wound itself, and clearly thought his throat had been cut. "They never come back!" he screamed. "I'm bleeding to death here!"

"You should," Helaine growled. "*Why* don't they come back?"

"Hey, I'm Pat Sajak!" Score protested. "You're Vanna White. I ask the questions, you turn the letters." Helaine didn't have a clue what he was talking about, and neither did their panicking captive.

"I don't know!" he howled, answering her question. "I just know that they go down into the mines to work—and they never come back."

"And *when* do they go down?" Score asked angrily.

"At daybreak," the man said. "They've already gone down. And they won't be coming back."

Score looked at Helaine. All the joking was gone from his voice now. "Pixel and Jenna will be down there," he said softly. "We've got to go help them. Now."

145

"If they are still alive," Helaine said bleakly. "I've been trying to contact them, and I can't get through to either of them. Score, we may be too late this time . . ."

11

Pixel sank beneath the waves, holding his breath, and feeling almost peaceful. Once under the surface, there were no waves to fight, and he almost seemed to be floating.

To his death . . .

He tried to get angry, or scared, or *anything* about this prospect, but all he could think was that he'd soon be feeding the fish. And fish, of course, could breathe happily underwater, even if he couldn't.

Wait a minute! Fish could breathe underwater because of their gills—they still needed oxygen, just like he did. Only they could extract it from the water, and he couldn't.

At least, not normally . . .

He clutched his beryl, which gave him command over the element of air, and thought very hard and clearly about what he wanted—a sort of bubble of air about his mouth and nose, so that he could breathe. A bubble that would keep renewing itself, and stay with him. A bubble that he wouldn't have to keep thinking about for it to continue . . .

Finally, he could hold his breath no longer, and he had to take the chance that his spell was working. He took a deep, gasping breath—and didn't drown. A few drops of sea water came into his mouth, but mostly it was pure, refreshing, life-giving air. It was working wonderfully!

Pixel's success cheered him up a lot, and he stopped being so lethargic in his thinking. Jenna's magic had given him enough of his strength back for him to work a bit of magic, at least. So now he wouldn't drown.

But he still might be eaten by sea monsters. And he didn't have a clue where he was, or where he should go. He looked around, and saw almost nothing in the dark waters. Glancing upward, he could see that there was a dim light above him that must be the surface of the sea. He wasn't even sure he could get up there. He was a bit more buoyant now, with air in his lungs, and he had stopped falling downward, but he was still pretty hopeless in the water. He regretted not learning to swim better.

Actually, this was quite like his VR explorations underwater. He could breath without effort, and the water was mildly warm, thankfully. But in virtual reality, he'd been able to move through the "water" just by thinking about it; he couldn't manage that here. But maybe he could figure something out . . . No, his power over air and fire weren't much use here, but what about finding and calling?

Finding! What an idiot he was! He could work out where to go from that. He gripped his ruby, and wanted to know where Jenna was. Immediately, a bright laser beam of light flashed from his hand and off to his right, vanishing into the distance. He grinned happily. Now, at least, he knew which direction to head. He started slowly swimming. It wasn't hard going, exactly, at least at first, but there were any number of problems.

First off all, since all he could see around him was about ten feet of water, it looked like he wasn't even moving—and he probably wasn't, much. How far did he have to go to get to Jenna? She was in a ship, traveling—well, he didn't know, but it had to be miles an hour. He was in the water, swimming, at maybe yards an hour . . . He'd never catch up this way, at least not in time to be of any use.

Besides, he wasn't used to swimming, and his clothes were all waterlogged and holding him back. He might not drown in the water, but he could die of exhaustion. He needed some other option, and that left calling. He switched to his jacinth, and thought hard: *I need help; is there anyone or anything that can give it to me?*

There was no immediate reply, of course, but he kept on swimming, and from time to time he touched the jacinth and sent the mental pleas for aid. He was getting very tired already, his muscles burning as he swam, but he wouldn't give up. He wouldn't! Poor Jenna must think he was dead, and she was so sweet and helpless, she'd need his help.

Something long, lean, and dangerous looking flashed by him. It was just a quick glimpse, a blur of motion, and then it was gone again.

A shark? Or whatever passed for sharks on this world? Pixel started to get very scared. His magic might be able to help him, but he had to be able to see or at least sense what he was fighting, and he couldn't do either. There was just this bubble of visibility about him, and nothing else.

Except another of the slim, fast forms—or maybe the same one back again—that zipped through his field of vision and was gone once more into the murkiness.

Pixel clutched his gemstone, and in almost feverish panic called again: *I need help—and I need it *fast!**

The shape darted in again, and this time hovered close by, staring at him. It wasn't a shark—it wasn't any kind of fish, in fact. It looked almost human, in a very odd way. Pixel stared at the creature in fascination, and it stared back, apparently equally bemused.

It was about his length, and a sort of dull gray color, with a lighter streak down its front. It had legs and arms instead of flippers, but these were streamlined, and had what looked like fins at the wrists and ankles. Gills in its neck pulsed as it regarded him, opening and closing in graceful motion. The face was almost human, too—with a nose of sorts, with two slits instead of nostrils. The mouth was small and delicate, but the teeth within were tiny and pointed, almost like a shark's. The eyes were large and dark, and regarded him with clear intelligence. The creature had no visible hair, nor clothing, though in its right hand it held a long, tapering spear. It was clearly intelligent!

But was it possible to communicate with this strange being? It looked almost like one of the Beastials he had met on Treen, a sort of dolphin-person. Surely, if it had a mind, he could make contact?

What manner of creature are you? a voice asked him, inside his head. *You look almost like those lumbering surface dwellers, yet you breath underwater and do not drown. Are you a ghost?*

Telepathy! Well, that made sense, Pixel realized. Now, if only this being could pick up his return thoughts . . . He focused clearly, and tried to project his message across. *No, I am no ghost. I *am* a surface dweller, and I can breath here only through magic.*

The creature darted off slightly, and then back, clearly startled. *You can speak!* it thought to him. *You may *look* like a surface dweller, but you're not like any one I have ever seen before. You're alive, for one thing. Most of the ones I've seen have been drowned—and most of those, half-eaten.*

Pixel tried not to think of that: there were certainly dangerous beasts in this alien sea! *You're not like anyone I've ever met before, either,* he thought back. *You're a mermaid. Or a merman. Or . . . Well, I'm not sure.*

He felt a peal of laughter in his mind. *You can't tell what I am? Do the females of your race look so different than me, then?*

A girl! Or, possibly, a woman, of course. *Quite a lot,* Pixel explained. *They have long hair, and . . . uh, other bodily shapes that kind of give them away.* This mer-being looked to be naked, which made sense underwater, where clothing was a drag. There was certainly no obvious indication that she was female, thank goodness! If there had been, Pixel would have been horribly embarrassed.

Hair? The mer-girl darted in closer, and touched the top of his head. *This is hair? It's like sea weed. What's it for?*

Actually, I'm not sure, Pixel admitted. *Keeping my head warm, I guess. Or preventing sunburn.*

What's sunburn?

Rather difficult to explain to someone who lives her whole life underwater, Pixel realized. *Look, I don't mean to be rude, but can you help me? I'm really not used to being in the sea, and I'm getting very tired swimming.*

The girl or woman swam around him, puzzled. *How can this be tiring?*

Maybe it isn't for you, but I'm not used to it.

She thought for a moment. *All right. I'll take you home with me, and maybe my parents will know what to do with you.* He had the mental picture of a big smile. *Just as long as they don't think you're another one of the strays I pick up and want to keep!*

So she was a girl, then! Pixel had suspected so from the way she talked. She might even be close to his own age, but since she looked so alien, it was hard to tell. *My name is Pixel,* he informed her.

And I'm Sorah, the mer-girl said. She swam next to him. *Hold on around my neck, and I'll swim for the both of us.*

Amazingly, even carrying him, Sorah could still swim like a torpedo, slicing through the water too fast for Pixel to even see what he was missing. She used her limbs and fins somehow, and even gentle kicks by her strong, muscular legs sent her flying. Pixel just hung on for dear life.

After about twenty minutes, Sorah slowed. *That's my home, just ahead,* she thought to Pixel. He glared into the gloom, but could see virtually nothing. Her eyes must be astonishingly well adapted to this environment! After a few moments, though, he started to make out lights ahead, and realized they were close to the sea bed.

Lights? Underwater? He wondered how the mer-folk managed that since fire couldn't burn down here. Then they were swimming together through a sort of underwater street, passing houses and other mer-beings. Some called greetings telepathically to Sorah; others seemed astonished at her latest "catch." Pixel examined them as much as he could in the gloom—even the lights from the homes didn't illuminate the murky waters much. He realized that Sorah was certainly the equivalent of a teenager—many of the mer-folk were larger than her, and just a few smaller. There was no obvious way to tell male and female apart, as all were slender and streamlined, with no hair. The markings on each one were slightly different—Sorah had a kind of white blaze on her throat, for example, that most of the others didn't have. Some had mark-ings on their arms, others had patches of color on their chests. Aside from that, they all looked remark-ably alike.

The homes were quite simple. They appeared to be almost crude blocks, made from what Pixel at first thought was stone, and then realized was some kind of coral. There were "windows" and "doors," but they were simply openings. Of course—glass couldn't be made underwater, and there were no trees in the depths. The only wood Sorah and her people would know about would be driftwood that floated down from the surface world.

We've arrived, Sorah informed him, and shot in through one of the openings into a small house. Pixel panicked, thinking that they were bound to hit a wall, but somehow Sorah managed to stop instantly, treading water in a pleasant room.

There was no furniture, just strands of kelp and seaweed that acted rather like doors or curtains, closing off other rooms. And the lights, he saw, were from luminescent sea mosses, gathered into balls and stuck onto the walls. It was extremely alien to him, but somehow rather homey.

There were three other mer-beings in the room—two larger than Sorah, and one smaller. This latter was staring at Pixel in astonishment. *Sea cows!* it finally exclaimed. *This has got to be the weirdest pet you've brought home yet, sis. Where did you get it?* He turned to the larger beings. *Can I get one, too, huh, can I? They'll all envy me at school.* He turned back to Sorah. *Is it house broken? I'm not going to clean up after it.*

Pixel heard Sorah's mental sigh. *My kid brother,* she explained. Ignoring him, she turned to her parents. *Mom, Dad—this is Pixel. He's from the surface world, and he's asking for help.*

The surface world? Sorah's father swam closer. *This is the first time I've seen one alive.* He peered closer. *It's very odd.*

He is quite nice, actually, Sorah replied.

Ignore his rudeness, Sorah's mother thought at Pixel. *He doesn't mean it. It's just a shock—we didn't know that your species could breathe underwater. They're usually drowned when we run across them.*

Well, most of them can't do it, Pixel explained. *I'm able to do magic, though, and this is something I worked out. I don't know if anyone else could do it, even my friends.*

Fascinating, the father said. *What's this magic?*

Later, dear, his wife replied. *Didn't Sorah say he was asking for help? Perhaps we should hear what his problem is before we start interrogating him?*

It took a while for Pixel to make them understand, mostly because they had never been above the surface for more than a few seconds at a time. They knew what boats were, of course, and that there was a sort of intelligence species living on top of the waters, but they didn't have a clue what pirates were, or slavery. But they were able to help him almost immediately.

This island you're after must be our mountain, Sorah's father said. *Our village is built on the slopes, and the peak extends up past the surface and into the sky. It's the only one around here, so it must be the one.*

Pixel grinned happily. *Then Jenna's probably very close! That's great. So if I follow the slope up, I'll be on the island, and I should be able to rescue her. Fantastic!*

Sorah's mother shook her head. *But it sounds so dangerous! And that island is not the safest place to be. In fact, we're thinking of abandoning our village and seeking somewhere new to settle. Only this has been our home for thousands of years.*

Why would you leave it then? Pixel asked.

Sea quakes, Sorah's father explained. *The mountain is volcanic, and there have always been tremors of sorts. But the heat warms our waters, making our homes pleasant, so we've always put up with them. Only lately the quakes have been more frequent and a lot stronger. A few houses have been destroyed, and fissures have formed in our streets. We may have no option but to abandon our homes.*

Pixel frowned. *Maybe there's some sort of connection,* he mused. *I mean, the pirates come to this island, and your quakes get worse. It's not likely to be a coincidence—but I can't see how they could be connected yet . . .*

Sorah's mother was indignant. *You think these men might have something to do with our troubles? That's terrible!*

Mom, he just got through telling you what stinkers they are, Sorah said. *They probably don't even know or care what they're doing to us.*

They probably don't even know you exist, Pixel said, an idea forming in his mind. *After all, the islanders never mentioned you.*

We don't have anything to do with the surface dwellers, Sorah's father said. *We can't breathe up there, and they can't breathe down here.*

Maybe I can help with that, Pixel said slowly. *If I can use magic to make myself breathe underwater, then I should be able to do the same to help you breathe above the surface. Do you think you could get a few people to volunteer to come with me at least to the surface to investigate what's happening?*

If it might help save our village, absolutely, Sorah's mother agreed. *You get some rest, and we'll see how many people will volunteer.*

I'm coming, Sorah said, firmly. *I found him, and he's *mine*.* Then she mentally blushed. *Uh, sorry, Pixel, I didn't mean it quite how it sounded. But we're friends, right? And I can help!*

Pixel laughed. *Yes, we're friends, and I'm sure you can help. Now, I've got the start of a plan. If all goes well, this should be easy.* Then he sighed. *And if I have my usual luck, it'll all get messed up, and we'll have to improvise as always.* But he had a small army of sorts to help him out now . . .

12

Jenna was still aching and sore, but at least the night's sleep and the meager breakfast they had been given had refreshed her a little bit. She no longer felt as if she were about to die. At least, not from her weakness. Whether the pirates would kill her was still an open question.

All of the prisoners had been fed, and then forced from their cell. In a ragged line, they were marched down a long, dank tunnel, heading into the bowels of the earth. No explanations were offered, and none of the prisoners dared to ask any questions. The pirates were joking amongst themselves, and from time to time striking a prisoner to keep them moving. Jenna found herself hating these men. How could they treat fellow human beings so cruelly, as if their lives meant nothing? Since she was a child, Jenna had been raised to believe that a human life was a sacred gift, and that anything she could do to help a person should be done. Perhaps she'd simply had wonderful parents—before they had died—but Jenna firmly believed that there was good in most people, and they were worth saving.

But these pirates—they didn't care for anyone else and were driven by greed. It was hard to believe that such depraved beings were once sweet, innocent children, with so much potential for good. Instead, they had surrendered to the darker sides of their nature, and were oppressing the weak to gain their own desires.

For the first time, Jenna found herself wishing she was more like Helaine. If the warrior girl was here now, she wouldn't be huddled over with the rest of the captives. No, she'd get a weapon from somewhere and somehow take on all of the guards, or die trying. For a noble, Helaine was actually quite considerate. And she certainly had a strong sense of right and wrong. Jenna discovered that she was almost missing the other girl. As for Pixel . . . She blotted out all thoughts of him. She wouldn't believe that he was dead, no matter how strong the evidence . . .

Their forced march down the passageways into the depths took them more than half an hour. It was getting hotter the farther they descended, so Jenna knew they must be getting closer to the power source of the volcano. She didn't know much science—she'd never been to school, after all, and the most her folks had been able to do was to teach her to read and write. She knew a lot about healing herbs and such simple remedies thanks to her mother's teaching, but very little about anything else. Pixel had been teaching her, but there was so much to learn! He *had* told her something about volcanoes, though . . . She searched through her memories . . . Ah, yes! They were filled with melted rock that forced its way through passages, and eventually burst from the top, flinging fire and destruction, sometimes for miles. Inside volcanoes, the liquid rock—lava, that was it!—flowed like rivers. She suspected that they had to be getting closer to one of those rivers.

Why would the pirates want them down here so deep? It had to be to work, and the work couldn't be anything other than digging. But what was there to dig for here?

Finally, they came into a large open space. The pirates had placed glowing torches of luminescent fungus all around the area. There were digging tools piled up in the corner, and Jenna could see that there was evidence of past digging in the walls.

"Alright, you pathetic creatures," Black Hawk growled. "Pick up those tools and start working. And I mean *now!*" The captives had little option. They shuffled over to the pile, each took a pick, or a shovel, and then stood there, wondering what to do. Jenna found herself with a pick and began milling around.

One of the pirates flicked his whip. "Get to work, you lazy dogs!" he howled, and sent the whip flicking out over the prisoners. It hit one of the men near Jenna, and he cried and stumbled, dropping his shovel. Blood was left in the mark of the lash.

"Get moving!" Black Hawk called out.

Jenna found she was more angry than frightened. "You haven't told anyone where, or what they're to do!" she snapped.

Black Hawk stared at her slowly, as if astonished by her spirit. "Oh, we've got a rebel here, have we?" he sneered. "Someone who hasn't learned her lesson? Well, you've seen what we do to people who ask questions." He curled his own whip, ready to strike.

"I didn't ask questions," Jenna said. "I made observations. You might get some work from these poor people if you told them where they should be and what you wish them to do."

"Oh, I might, might I?" The whip lashed out, and caught Jenna across the biceps. She cried out and dropped the pick, agony burning across her arm. "Don't get sassy with me, girlie—it's not worth it." Then he glared at the prisoners. "That far wall—get along there, and start digging at it. Move, or you'll all get whipped." He turned back to Jenna. "Pick up your tool and join them."

Jenna glared back at him. Oh for a sword, and the knowledge of how to use it! But she had neither. Instead, she used her carnelian to start her arm healing, and did as she was ordered.

As the workers set to, flakes of stone came from the wall of rock, littering the ground and making work harder. Those slaves with shovels moved what they could aside. Jenna worked, knowing she would be whipped again if she didn't, and tried to puzzle this all out.

The pirates weren't *looking* for anything. They were just watching the diggers to make sure they worked. Whatever was cut from the wall was thrown into large piles of scrap. If they were after gold or gems, surely they would have someone sifting through the debris? So why were they forcing slaves to dig a tunnel if it wasn't to find something?

Pixel had always taught her to try and be logical. A tear trickled down her face at the thought of how much she missed him and his gentle wisdom. She wiped it on the back of her dirty hand. She wasn't going to give in and believe he was dead! She wasn't going to weep! Think, she ordered herself. Do what he would do. Make him proud of you!

Right, so the pirates weren't digging this tunnel to look for anything. The only other possibility, then, was that they were digging it to get at something. But what was down here? Only the river of lava, and why would they be after that? It made no sense.

Despite the heat, she felt a sudden chill. It made a sudden, terrible sense! *That* was why they always needed new slaves! Once they dug through to the lava, the heat would kill the diggers . . . But what possible use could the pirates have for a flow of lava? There had to be another piece to this puzzle she simply didn't know yet.

But there was one clear thing that she *did* know—she couldn't allow this work to go on! Every blow, every second, was bringing everyone here closer to a horrible death! Perhaps Helaine was the warrior, and she was the healer, but this was a time for fighting and not medicine. It was time for her to take action.

Fine, but *how*? She had no weapons, and her gemstones weren't really suited to fighting. They fit her nature, which was gentle and healing, neither of which were of much use in this situation. Her power of persuasion might work—on one person at a time. But the moment she tried to convince one man, the rest were bound to attack her.

Then it had to be invisibility. She would use that as her weapon. If she was invisible, then the pirates wouldn't be able to see her. She might be able to steal a weapon . . . And do *what*? Get herself killed? Her only other hope were a few spells she'd learned from Pixel. She could make a fireball and toss it—but that would burn someone up horribly, and she wasn't sure she could bring herself to kill even these pirates. And if she hesitated once she started, then *they* would kill her for certain.

Invisibility . . . She was sure that was the key, if she could only work out how to use it! As she hacked at the wall, she glanced around—and realized something. The pirates were all hanging back from the workers, close to the exit from this cavern. Of course they were! The moment the slaves cut through the wall, lava would flow, and anyone in its path would die! The pirates were ready to flee for their lives at a second's notice.

Now she knew what to do!

She turned to Lahra, working beside her. "Talk to the others," she whispered. The pirates couldn't hear them at this distance. "Tell them to get ready to fight for their lives."

"We'll be killed," Lahra whispered back.

"We'll die if we don't," Jenna said, and explained quickly about the lava. "I have a plan, and I'm going to start it in a few minutes. It's essential everyone helps."

"All right," Lahra agreed. Then she turned to the worker beside her, and started to pass on the message as she worked.

Jenna gave Lahra enough time to have spread the word to a number of their fellow prisoners. It would be better if not everyone knew that something was up, so that their panic would be real, and help fool the pirates. Then she cautiously tapped into the power of her obsidian, and started the magic to create invisibility—not on her or her fellow workers, but on the wall that they were working on. She didn't really know how thick it was, but, judging from the rise in heat since they had started, it couldn't be too thick . . . She could only pray that she had the strength to make something that massive invisible . . .

Now! She lashed out with all of her power.

The wall appeared to dissolve before them, and the lava beyond was suddenly visible, surging and flowing.

"Lava!" Jenna screamed, and turned to run, as if in panic. Several of the prisoners did the same, some knowing that this had to be a trick, others thinking it was for real.

This was the second the pirates had been waiting for, of course. As soon as they saw the lava, they turned and fled, not wanting to be enveloped in the flow, and leaving their prisoners to die.

Jenna and three of the others managed to catch up with the last of the fleeing pirates. Unused to fighting as she was, Jenna put all of her rage into the blows she struck. She still held her pick, but couldn't bring herself to kill even a pirate. Breaking a few bones, on the other hand, was tremendously satisfying. Crying, terrified, several of the pirates fell. Jenna led the charge up the corridor after the remaining guards, who finally sensed that something was wrong. They slowed, and then turned, puzzled. Their confusion turned to anger, though, when they saw that a handful of the prisoners were chasing them.

"It's some kind of a trick!" Black Hawk yelled. "I don't know how they did it, but there's no lava flowing! Get them!"

Now they were in for trouble! Chasing scared, fleeing pirates was one thing, but facing angry armed pirates was another. Jenna's little force faltered and then drew back behind her. Jenna did a quick count—there were still eight pirates and Black Hawk himself on their feet. In a pitched battle, there was no way her puny force could win.

But backing down would be certain death, both for them and the rest of the prisoners left behind. Jenna clutched her pick more tightly. Maybe now she'd have no choice but to kill . . .

"Don't retreat," she called to her companions. "We'll be killed when the lava *does* break through if you do. Would you sooner be burned to death, or fight for your freedom?"

Lahra stood beside her. "I'll fight," she said, simply, even though there was fear in her voice. The rest of the group muttered almost inaudibly, but none fled.

"They're just untrained scum!" the captain yelled to his men. "They'll be easy to kill."

"But we won't be," said a fresh voice from behind the pirates. Jenna's heart leaped as she recognized that voice—Helaine! Black Hawk and his men looked back, and saw in the corridor behind them that Helaine and Score were ready, grinning slightly.

"Is this a private fight?" Score asked. "Or can anyone join in?"

"Two more children," Black Hawk sneered. "There's nothing to be scared of."

"Oh yes, there is," Helaine said grimly. She moved forward, sword at the ready. The closest pirate lunged at her. She blocked the blow, parried, and then slashed out. The blow broke through his guard and slashed through his arm. With a scream, he fell aside, and Helaine pressed on.

"Come on!" Jenna yelled, and she rushed forward, raising her pick.

The next few seconds were a complete blur to her. She struck out, again and again, at anyone who came anywhere near her. She heard yells of pain, and the sounds of blows being struck, but she was so angry at the pirates and pleased to see her friends that she was working on a tremendous buzz.

"Hold it!" said a familiar voice. "I surrender!"

Jenna paused, and wiped the hair from her eyes, and she realized that she had just been about to brain Score. Sweating and panting, she glanced around. All of the pirates were down, except for Black Hawk, and he was locked in combat with Helaine.

"I'm sorry," she gasped. "I guess I got kind of carried away."

"I'll say," Score said, approval strong in his voice. "You're quite the little rebel leader, aren't you?"

Jenna looked at Helaine, who was hacking away at Black Hawk's sword. "Shouldn't we help her?"

"Come on, you know better than that," Score said. "If we even try, she'll be so mad at us she'd beat us up next. Besides, this guy is an amateur; she's going to cream him."

Jenna wasn't quite as sure as Score, and couldn't help worrying about Helaine. The pirate captain was twenty years older than her, and a hundred pounds heavier. His blows were stronger, and his strength greater. But she realized that Score was correct—Helaine was fighting with a grin on her face. She managed somehow to avoid all the killing blows Black Hawk tried, and was instead slashing at him, getting through his guard and leaving him with a number of cuts. Finally, in one swift move, she caught his blade, whirled her own, and his sword went flying.

"Enough!" he exclaimed, defeated. "I surrender."

"Told you," Score smirked at Jenna. "That's my girl."

It was over, Jenna suddenly realized. She was safe again, and with her friends. "Oh, Score, I'm so glad to see you!" she cried. She threw her arms around him and hugged him, and then kissed his cheek.

"Remind me to save your life more often," he joked. "Of course, only when Pixel isn't around to get jealous." Then he blinked. "Uh, where is he, by the way?"

In all of the fighting, Jenna had almost been able to forget. Now, though, a tear rolled down her cheek. "Oh, Score—I think he must be dead . . . The pirates threw him overboard at sea yesterday. There was a monster, and even if that didn't get him, he can't swim, and . . ." She started to break down, sobbing.

Two strong arms grabbed her and held her. She thought it was Score until she heard Helaine's voice in her ear. "Pixel is tougher than he seems," she said gently. "I don't think he'd die that easily."

Jenna wiped at her eyes and nose with the back of her hand. "You really believe that?" she asked hopefully. "I want to, but it seems so hopeless."

"Hopeless?" Score laughed. "That's Pixel's middle name!" He glanced at Helaine. "Why don't you try reaching him again?" He looked at Jenna. "But if she doesn't get through, it doesn't necessarily mean anything bad. Just that he's likely out of range, okay?"

"I won't panic," she promised, smiling as bravely as she could.

Helaine gripped her agate, and concentrated. Then the frown lifted from her face, and she grinned. "I got through," she reported. "It seems he's on his way here with a small army of his own."

"Too late," Score laughed.

A huge weight lifted off Jenna's soul. "He's alive . . ." she breathed, thankfully. She went weak, and almost fell. Score grabbed her, and helped her to stand.

"Don't get too used to holding onto her," Helaine warned Score.

"You're only jealous," Score mocked.

"Pixel will be too," Helaine replied. "And he's got an army with him, remember."

"Spoil sport," Score complained. Jenna realized that both of them were only joking, of course. She threw her arms around Helaine, and hugged her.

"I'm so glad to see you," she said honestly.

Helaine looked surprised—and almost pleased. "Well, it's not too much of a pain to see you, either," she admitted. "I guess I did kind of worry about you."

"And I only managed to do what I did by trying to do what I thought you'd do," Jenna told her.

"You were very brave," Helaine said, somewhat grudgingly.

"Wow, all this love flying around," Score said. "It's quite giddying. Next you'll want to go shopping at the mall together, and try on each other's sweaters."

Jenna had no idea what he was talking about, but that was pretty much normal for Score. "Now what do we do?" she asked.

"Now," said Oracle's voice from down the tunnel, "you start to *really* worry."

The three of them looked around. Their odd friend was standing there, back where the rest of the prisoners remained. He was looking quite concerned.

"It's that long streak of misery," Score complained. "Hey, I've got a bone to pick with you—you *knew* about all of this, didn't you? You conned us!"

"I knew all about this—and more," Oracle corrected him. "These pirates aren't your real foes here." He pointed further back. "*They* are."

Jenna gasped as she saw what he was indicating.

Tall flames were burning in the corridor—seven or eight feet tall, there were three of them. Her skin crawled, though, as she realized that there was nothing there for them to be burning. The corridor was simply solid rock . . .

The three flames were separate and distinct. Each was a slightly different shade of red or orange.

And each of them moved slowly forward towards them . . .

13

Score groaned as he saw what appeared to be some weird kind of living flames advancing down the rock-hewn corridor toward their small party. The flames were dancing and flickering, but somehow managing to move without anything to feed them.

"Don't let them get any closer!" Black Hawk called out. The fear in his voice was quite apparent. "They'll burn us to death!"

"Which is fine for you," Score snapped. "But I think those of us on the good guys team deserve a little better." He glared at Oracle. "Do those things speak English? *Can* they speak at all?"

"They have no mouths or voice boxes," Oracle answered. "And their minds are quite different from yours. There is little point of contact."

"There's *some* point," Score pointed out. "These scuzzy pirates somehow struck a deal with them." He scowled at Black Hawk. "Which I'm going to want to hear about really soon. But for now—any clues on how to stop these things from burning us up? Pixel's the one who can control fire, and he's conspicuous by his absence."

"They have different senses than you," Oracle said. "They may not even be able to detect that you're alive—or even here."

"So why are they advancing on us?" Helaine asked. "And why don't I have my usual feeling of danger that I get when I'm being attacked?"

"They aren't attacking you," Oracle replied. "They're simply heading for heat. These tunnels are too cold for them. They need the gentle warmth of lava to stay alive."

"And they can't dig through cold rock to get it," Jenna said suddenly. "That's why they needed humans to dig to it for them."

It made sense at last. Score turned to Helaine. "Communications is your gift. Get your agate working—fast!" The beings were only about fifteen feet away now, and he could feel the heat radiating from their bodies.

Helaine nodded, and gripped her gemstone. She concentrated, and then gasped. "I can . . . *feel* them," she whispered. "But they're so . . . alien. I don't think they understand me." They were still advancing.

"Time to retreat," Score muttered. He turned to Black Hawk. "Gather up your fallen men, and let's move."

"Leave them," Black Hawk urged. "They're not important."

Score was disgusted. "You're not at the top of my 'Ten Best Employers Of The Year' list," he growled. "If we leave them, I'm breaking your legs and leaving you with them. Now pick them up!" He turned to the frightened islanders. "Help him with them. Nobody gets left behind. We'll cover your retreat."

"How?" Jenna asked him, all too practically. "What can we do to fight them?"

"Hey, I'm making this up as I go along," Score complained. "Your boyfriend is the brains of our outfit, and he's not here."

"So we fall back on Score's specialty," Helaine added. "Dumb luck. Emphasis on *dumb*."

Score glanced around and saw that the pirates were all being carried or dragged away. "Helaine, you'd better go with them and make sure Black Hawk doesn't stage a coup, or something."

"You need me here," she protested.

"We don't need to be watching our backs," he pointed out. "Besides, someone has to get the other freed slaves organized, and you're the bossiest person I know."

She grinned. "Try not to get killed."

"With so much to look forward to?" he asked her. "Not a chance. Beat it." He didn't look back as she left with the others. Instead he smiled at Jenna. "You still sure you like being a member of our group?" he asked her.

"Oh, yes," she replied. "You may do it strangely, but you fight for what is right. And I do have an idea." She turned to Oracle. "Those beings have trouble with things colder than themselves?"

"Yes," he agreed. "They can't pass through stone or anything like that."

She nodded, and then swallowed nervously. "Then I *think* I can stop them." She was clutching her aquamarine hard. Then she walked forward, deliberately into the path of the leading flame.

"Hey, have you gone crazy?" Score cried.

"I hope not," she said, without looking back. "I have the power of survival, remember? I only hope that it's strong enough to protect me." She sounded resolute, but scared, and Score couldn't blame her.

"Will it work?" he asked Oracle, urgently, afraid that he'd see her suddenly burn to a crisp.

"On a Rim World?" Oracle shrugged. "We shall find out in moments."

"With luck, only her clothes will burn up," Score said, cheering slightly at the thought.

"You have an obsession with seeing the skin of girls," Jenna called back. "It's very unhealthy."

"Yeah, you can slap my face any time you like," Score told her. "*If* she survives," he added to himself. He was terrified for her, but couldn't think of anything he could do that might help.

Jenna was sweating; her hair was plastered to her head and neck, and her clothes were drenched. But she moved resolutely forward, gasping slightly with each step she took. Then, finally, she and the first living flame met. With a final deep breath, she walked forward and into the fire.

The redness enveloped her, surging slightly. Score's heart thumped madly in his chest as he was certain she'd flare up and burn. He'd never forgive himself—or the flames—if that happened . . .

But she didn't burn. Instead, the flame flickered and seemed to cool. Then it moved back. The other two flames had halted also, and were wavering where they floated.

"She's too cold for them," Oracle said reverently. "That is one brave, foolish, and amazing girl."

"Isn't she?" Score agreed. "So, we've got their attention—what do we do next?"

"I can . . . hear them," Jenna said quietly. "The one I touched realizes that there is something here. I think it can sense my mind. It's hard to understand what it is saying, though. It seems amazed that I can live, being so cold."

Sweat was pouring down Score's face and back, partly from the heat and partly from fear for her. "Jenna, don't hang around. You've stopped them, so come away."

"No, I'm okay, Score, really I am." Jenna looked back and smiled slightly. "They don't mean us any harm."

"Yeah, but their not meaning us any harm can still kill us."

"I'm going to try and communicate with them," Jenna told him. "Be quiet, please."

"You're learning from Helaine," Score muttered. "Or is it just that all girls are bossy?" Then he shut up, and waited, watching. Jenna was focused on her task and ignoring everything else. Finally, she broke contact and slowly walked back toward him. Score ran as close to the fire beings as he dared, and helped support her as she walked unsteadily back.

She was shaking, and drenched in sweat, but she looked relatively happy. "I think I got through to it," she said. "It's hard to be sure that either of us really understood each other—they're just so *alien*."

"Well, what did ET have to say?" Score demanded. "Is he going home?"

"This *is* his home," Jenna said. "This was their planet, long before humans arrived. They're very ancient—tens of thousands of years old, at the least. They live within the heart and heat of a volcano, basking in the warmth. But as this world cooled, their beings died out. There are now no more than a few hundred left, all living inside this island. But they couldn't get at the lava, and were slowly dying.

"Then someone came to them and offered them a bargain. The pirates would dig fresh tunnels to the lava, so that the flames could live. In return, the flames would bring gemstones and leave them in the passageways. The pirates would collect the gems as payment. The flames had no idea that slaves were digging the tunnel, and dying as they did so. I'm only the second human they've ever talked with."

Score was getting good and mad now. "And who was the first?" he asked.

"They don't know." Jenna shook her head. "We're so alien to them, we probably all look alike to them, as they seem to do to us."

"It couldn't have been one of the pirates," Oracle pointed out. "It would require magical strength to communicate with the flame creatures."

"And the pirates aren't that familiar with magic," Score agreed. "They know it exists, but not one of them can use it."

"So there's somebody else, someone manipulating both sides of this deal," Score said grimly. "Someone who isn't bothered by a lot of deaths. Another evil magician."

"But where is he—or she?" Oracle asked.

"We need Pix to do a search," Score said. "I hope he hurries up and gets here. A magician who can survive contact with these flames is going to be a tough cookie to crumble." He thought for a moment. "Okay, Jenna—do you think the flames will back off for a while, to give us time to think?"

"Uh . . . no," she replied. "Score, they're *dying*. They need the heat, and without it they'll perish. They're sorry, but they have to have that lava."

"Uh-oh . . ." Score was starting to get scared again. "And how do they intend to go about getting it?"

Jenna bit at her lower lip, and couldn't meet his eyes. "Now that they know humans exist, they are going to force them to dig through to the lava."

"It will kill them!"

"They know that," Jenna answered. "But they feel it is their survival against ours—and, like so many beings, they wish to live."

"Do they indeed?" Score was good and mad now. "You know, I was just starting to feel sorry for them. Now, forget it. If it's going to be like that, then I'm going to start stomping on some fires . . ."

"What are you going to do?" Jenna asked him, startled.

"I'm going to become a one-man fire brigade," Score vowed. "I always did think I'd look hot in leather boots and a silly helmet." He gripped his chrysolite. "Don't forget—I have power over water, and water can put out fire . . ." He stared at the hovering flames. "Do you think you could get that across to them?"

"I don't think they would care," she replied honestly. "They're *desperate*—and desperate beings don't act rationally. Anyway, even if you could put out these three fires, there are still a few hundred more of them, and you wouldn't be able to put them all out. I think it may be time to retreat—Helaine and the others must have reached safety by now."

"*Temporary* safety," Score reminded her. "And it's so good not to be the first one to suggest retreating. Let's go." The flames didn't attempt to stop them; they simply hovered where they burned. Score was glad when he could no longer see them.

They hurried back to the surface, where Helaine was waiting grimly for them. All of the pirates were now locked in their own holding cell, and the islanders had vanished.

"I sent them down to the ship," Helaine explained. "Told them to get it ready to sail at a moment's notice. If there's trouble, we might be able to escape that way."

"Why don't we just go now?" Jenna asked. "I don't think there's anything we can do here, anyway."

Oracle frowned. "What about the living flames?" he asked. "They will die out soon, with nobody left to dig through to the lava for them."

Score jerked his thumb toward the cell. "There's always the pirates—a taste of their own medicine might be poetic justice."

Helaine shook her head. "They might deserve it, but can you just leave them here to die?"

Score considered. "Maybe not," he finally agreed. "And Oracle is right—we have to do something about those flames—but what?"

"I have an idea," said Pixel from the cave mouth. Jenna gave an excited squeal, ran to him, threw her arms around him, and kissed him.

Score scowled at Helaine. "How come you never greet me like that?"

"You don't return from the dead," she replied. "And I thought I wasn't your girlfriend anyway?"

"I thought you were dead," Jenna babbled to Pixel. "No, I mean, I *didn't* think it—but I was afraid of it."

"I know what you mean," Pixel said, smiling happily. "And I almost was. But Sorah and her folks helped me." He gestured at the strange beings with him. Score stared at them in surprise—they looked like humanized dolphins, with large, expressive eyes and a mouth filled with tiny, pointed teeth. Pixel told his story, and then they brought him up-to-date.

"You said you had an idea," Score reminded him, finally. He was glad the brains of the group was back to take over for the moment.

"I do," Pixel said. He turned to the smallest of the three beings with him. "Sorah, can you and your parents get the rest of your people to dig down that trench I pointed out to them? But don't break through." The three mer-folk nodded, and then ran back toward the sea.

"Two questions," Helaine said, beating Score to the punch. "First, I thought you said these mer-folk can't live out of water? Second, what are you up to?"

"They can't, normally," Pixel explained. "But I just reversed the magic I used on myself. I helped them to keep water in their systems, so that they can breathe air for a short while. They're really nice folks, and I hope they and the islanders can become friends."

"Your plan . . ." Score prompted.

"The mer-folk have found a place where the crust of the volcano is quite thin underwater," Pixel said. "I'm getting them to make it thinner, so that with a little effort, we can puncture the shell, and let the sea flood in."

Jenna gasped. "But that would boil the water . . . and cool the lava."

"Right," Pixel agreed. "It would drop the temperature here to far below the level that the living flames need to stay alive. It's a threat we can use to make them do what we want."

"Great." Score blinked. "And what do we want?"

"Come with me and see," Pixel suggested. He started off down the corridor.

Score stared after him. "Great—he's been back from the dead less than half an hour, and already I'm thinking of strangling him. He has no right to be mysterious—that's Oracle's job."

14

Helaine was glad that the four of them were reunited again. She didn't know quite what Pixel had in mind, but she had faith that it would be clever. This was what he was best at. She trotted along with Score and Jenna after Pixel; Oracle blinked out of existence, presumably going on ahead. The fire beings couldn't hurt him since he didn't have a body to burn.

"I really don't like this business of another mad magician on the loose,"

Score muttered to her as they went deeper into the caves again.

"Not so mad," she told him. "One of the pirates was scared enough to talk. He told me that the magician set this up on a business basis—taking ten percent of the gems that the flame things brought. The problem is, the only pirate the magician ever dealt with was Black Hawk, and he's not talking. At least, not yet. So I don't even know if our foe is male or female."

"Or even if he or she is our foe," Score replied. "After all, whoever it is seems to be operating on a Rim World, far, far away from us."

"Come on, Score," she pointed out. "This is a magician without ethics—setting up the islanders to be enslaved and killed. And the gems are obviously so he or she can do stronger magic. What are the odds that we won't run up against this magician sooner or later?"

Score sighed. "Right; with our luck, it's inevitable. Well, when we get back, we'll do our good cop, bad cop routine on the Pirate King. I think he'll believe you're a homicidal maniac pretty easily."

"Is my acting that good?" she asked him.

"You were acting?"

Typical Score—an insult. She ignored it, knowing he didn't really mean it.

They came to a halt as they saw the flames moving slowly up the corridor toward them. Helaine gripped her agate, and concentrated. The flames must have learned something from their contact with Jenna, because now she could make out their thoughts. They were still alien, but at least a little more understandable.

Warmth . . . they were hissing. *Need warmth. Get it for us . . .*

No, she sent back. *That we shall not.*

Need warmth to live, the flames insisted. *Give it, or we consume you all.*

That won't get you the warmth, she informed them. Then she expanded her magic to allow Pixel and the others to join in.

You will lose completely soon, Pixel told them flatly. *I have an army of helpers readying a tidal wave. It will cool all the lava near the surface, and you will *never* get warmth again.*

You'll kill us! the flames protested.

*No," Pixel replied. *I offer you a chance to live.*

How? they demanded.

Pixel looked around. "Where's Oracle when I need him?" he complained. The dark figure slipped through the wall to stand beside him. "Right, Oracle—tell me: is there a Rim World that can be reached via a portal that's really close to its sun? One that's incredibly hot?"

Oracle nodded. "Yes, indeed—Brakt. I see what you have in mind. You want me to have Shanara open a portal from this world to that, so the flames can move there."

"Right." Pixel turned back to the flames. *This world will inevitably become too cold for you,* he informed them. *Opening the lava tunnels only delays the inevitable. But if you move to Brakt, you'll have a world where you will not be cold for millions of years.*

But this world is our home, the fires protested. *We cannot leave.*

You have no choice, Pixel said gently. *I know it can be a shock to leave the place you've always lived. It was for all of us, too—but we did it. And we love it now. I'm sure the same will happen with you. Besides, you really don't have any choice. You'll die sooner or later if you stay here.*

We will talk, the flames said, and cut off communications.

Jenna looked worried. "Do you think it will work?" she asked.

Pixel shrugged. "It's their only logical choice," he said. "But there's nothing forcing them to chose logically. We can only wait and see."

Helaine patted his shoulder. "You've done well, though," she said. "And, that reminds me . . ." She swallowed, and forced herself to face Jenna. This wasn't going to be easy, but it had to be done. "I was wrong about you," she admitted. "You have acted very bravely, and risked your life several times to do what is right. I apologize for my bad behavior and wish to be friends." She held out her hand.

"Not yet," Jenna said. Helaine was annoyed, and felt her anger building again. She had apologized and offered friendship, and this peasant was refusing her? Jenna swallowed hard. "I was wrong about you, too. You may have been born a noble, but I've seen that you act well, and from your heart. I owe you just as much of an apology." She sighed. "Now—perhaps we can be friends." She held out her own hand.

Helaine realized she'd been letting her anger win again. Jenna was actually being noble and sweet. She took the other girl's hand and shook it. "It may take me a while to actually be nice to you," she warned.

"And it may be a while before I stop snapping at you," Jenna said. "But we can overcome it."

"We were born what we were," Helaine said. "But we do not have to remain it. I am pleased we are trying to overcome the past."

"Way to go, girls!" Score said enthusiastically. "You have no idea the stress your fighting was putting Pix and I through."

Jenna turned to Pixel. "Poor boy!" she said sympathetically. "Were you really stressed out?"

He nodded. "My girl and one of my best friends hating one another? You bet."

Jenna kissed his cheek. "I'll have to make it up to you later," she promised him.

Score turned to Helaine. "Are you going to make it up to me?" he asked.

"You'll get what's coming to you," Helaine promised.

Then the flames spoke. *Decision reached,* their voices said. *We will go.*

"Splendid!" Pixel said happily. "Right, Oracle, off you go to get things started. We'll work everything out on this end . . ."

A short while later, Helaine stood with the others, watching as a procession of the tall, quivering flames floated down the rocky corridor and through the black gash that was the portal to Brakt. Everything seemed to have worked out well. There were just a few details to settle, and this would all be over.

Then the sense of danger tingled throughout her body. She whipped out her borrowed sword, and looked around. "Trouble," she hissed.

Black Hawk came rushing to where they stood, carrying a sword of his own. "Did you think my own jail could hold me?" he cried. "Stupid kids—you've ruined my plans! But I'm not going to rot in a cell for the rest of my life."

Helaine laughed. "Then come to me, and die swiftly," she mocked him. She had no intention of actually killing him, but beating the stuffing out of him would be fun. She'd taken him once, and knew she could again.

So did he, obviously. He shook his head. "He who fights and runs away lives to fight another day," he called back. Then he ran towards them.

Helaine fell back, ready to take any blow he might give, but there was none. He rushed past her.

"No!" Pixel yelled, alarmed. "Not the portal!"

"You can't stop me!" the pirate howled, and threw himself through it.

Helaine was shocked. "Can he survive there?"

Pixel shook his head. "Not a chance," he replied. "The surface temperature there is almost 500 degrees. He would have burnt to death the second he stepped through."

"No big loss," Score commented. "If anyone deserved such a fate, it was that scum, considering what he did."

"Maybe," Helaine said. "But he was the only one who could tell us about the magician, remember?"

"Big deal. That can wait."

Helaine shrugged. Maybe Score was right. In any event, she was certain that the magician would show his or her hand again some time, and then they would face off. There was no point in worrying about it now.

The final flames slipped through the portal and it closed down. Oracle smiled.

"Well, you four have done it again," he said. "You sorted out the situation. I knew you could."

"That reminds me," Score said. "We've got a bone to pick with you—you set us up, didn't you? We asked for a holiday and you sent us on a mission."

"You didn't *really* want a holiday, did you?" asked Oracle innocently. "You were all getting bored on Treen— you needed something to occupy your minds. And look on the bright side—Helaine and Jenna have become friends. That was something else you wanted . . ." His voice trailed off as he saw that Score wasn't appeased. "Well, maybe it's time I left, too." He promptly vanished.

"Coward," Score muttered. He turned to Pixel. "You know, if you were half as smart as you think you are, you'd figure out some way we could get back at him."

Pixel shrugged. "I'll have to think about it."

"Well, now that it's all over, why don't we *finally* hit the beach?" Score suggested. He put his arm around Pixel's shoulder and led him off. "Maybe I can talk a couple of these Harvester girls into wearing bikinis."

"I had Shanara conjure one up for me," Helaine said. "Just out of curiosity."

Helaine held up two strips. They were of some sort of bright blue fabric, and there wasn't much to them. Jenna stared at them.

"It would be immoral to allow anyone to see you wearing so little!" Jenna protested, blushing furiously.

"Not *anyone*, according to Score," Helaine replied. "*Everyone*. On his world, girls our age think nothing of dressing like this, and parading in public."

"They must be crazy," Jenna muttered.

"It's another world," Helaine explained, patiently. "We can't judge what they do there by the standards of our planet. Remember—we are shaped by our pasts, but not bound to them."

Jenna nodded. "You're right." She took a deep breath. "Well, if you are going to wear that in public, then I shall wear one, too—and hope I don't die of shame."

"Thank you for your support," Helaine said softly to Jenna. "But I do not think it will be needed. Score has behaved exceptionally, and I think I owe him some enjoyment. But *only* him."

She followed the pathway until she caught up with Score. She swallowed, forcing her pride and shame down. "Score . . . I have decided that I shall wear a bikini for you."

"Hey!" Score exclaimed, looking delighted. "Now let's get on with . . ." His voice trailed off, and his eyes narrowed in suspicion. "Hey! Wait a minute!" He pointed an accusing finger at her. "You always said that only your husband would get to see that much of you!"

"Yes, I did," Helaine confirmed.

"Oh, no!" Score protested. "If this is some kind of attempt to sucker me into saying you're my fiancé or

something, then I *don't* want to see you in a bikini!"
He turned and fled.

Pixel put his arm around Jenna's shoulders. "Well, I
for one like the way you dress. Both of you are very at-
tractive, no matter what clothes you have on."

Jenna grinned back at him, and then held her hand
out to Helaine. "May I have that bikini, if you have
no further use for it?" Helaine handed it over, raising
one eyebrow.

"Are you trying to trap me into proposing to you?"
Pixel asked Jenna.

"Do I have to trap you?" she teased him.

"No . . . I don't think so."

Jenna kissed his cheek. "That's what I thought. So
if I *do* wear this, it won't be a trap—but a reward." She
grinned at Helaine. "Of course, I haven't promised I'll
wear it . . ." The two of them wandered off together.

Love! Helaine sighed. Actually, they were kind of
cute, in a nauseating sort of way. She was rather glad
that nothing affected *her* like that! She would never
make a fool of herself for any male—not even Score.

She wandered slowly after the others. Well, with all
of this worked out now, maybe they would finally get
that holiday . . . This island was really rather nice, and
it could be very restful here. She glanced down at the

frilly shirt and pants she was wearing. On the other hand, she would like to get back into some proper clothing again.

She couldn't help thinking that there was something they had all forgotten, though. Oh well, time to say goodbye to the islanders, who would be able to make their way home now. And to those odd, pleasant mer-folk that Pixel had found.

But what else?

She blinked as she emerged into the sunlight again, after so long underground. Pixel and Jenna were strolling down toward the pier, hand in hand. Score was about twenty yards ahead of them, lost in his own thoughts. Helaine smiled. They were her good friends— even Jenna, she realized. She'd been stubborn and arrogant with the girl, and she felt ashamed of her behavior. She'd never really had a girlfriend before—her sisters were all boring, obsessed with dresses and making a good marriage. And there had been no other girl of her age and station in her father's castle. It might be kind of fun having a female friend around.

A yell from behind her made her spin around. Pouring from the mouth of the cave was a bunch of the pirates, waving swords.

Now she knew what she'd been trying to remember! If Black Hawk had freed himself, obviously his men had, too . . .

And she'd left her borrowed sword behind . . .

She turned and bolted after the other three. This was all Score's fault! Him and his obsession with girls in bikinis! She was going to beat the stuffing out of him— just as soon as they got away from these pirates . . .

The story continues in
BOOK OF REALITY

To Write to the Author

If you wish to contact the author or would like more information about this book, please write to the author in care of Llewellyn Worldwide and we will forward your request. Both the author and publisher appreciate hearing from you and learning of your enjoyment of this book. Llewellyn Worldwide cannot guarantee that every letter written to the author can be answered, but all will be forwarded. Please write to:

John Peel
℅ Llewellyn Worldwide
2143 Wooddale Drive, Dept. 0-7387-0748-1
Woodbury, MN 55125-2989, U.S.A., Earth, The Diadem

Please enclose a self-addressed stamped envelope or one dollar
to cover mailing costs. If you are writing from outside the
U.S.A., enclose an international postal reply coupon.

Many of Llewellyn's authors have websites with additional information and resources. For more information, please visit our website at:

www.llewellyn.com

ENTER THE DIADEM

Score is a street kid from New York City. Helaine is a fierce girl warrior from the medieval planet Ordin. Pixel lives in Virtual Reality on the futuristic world of Calomir.

Abandoned on a perilous world, the trio's survival depends on finding out who—or what—is drawing them deeper into the Diadem, a multi-level universe of magic, danger, and betrayal.

Find out more at http://teen.llewellyn.com

ENCOUNTERS

Cassie Strange is the only normal person in her family. . .

Her dad is a TV celebrity who debunks the paranormal on his own TV show. Her naturalist mom once wore a grass dress, complete with worms. Her genius brother is an aspiring (and annoying) actor, and her little sister Amber has a secret way of talking to animals. As if that weren't bad enough, Cassie's family can't seem to go anyplace without having some sort of strange encounter . . .

Book 1
Oh No! UFO!

What would you do if aliens kidnapped your little sister?

Book 2
Shamrocked!

A treasure map and secret underground world can mean only one thing—look out for leprechauns!

Book 3
Sea Switch

Something fishy is up when Cassie meets a rebellious mermaid who's been making waves in her under- water world.

TEMPTING

FATE?

Follow Juniper, Anne, and Gena—
the founding members of the Fortune Tellers Club—as they use
Tarot cards, crystal balls, and other
cool fortune telling tools to solve
mysteries and save lives.

Books in the Fortune Tellers
Club series:

The Lost Girl

Playing with Fire

The Magic Shades '

Secrets of Lost Arrow

Hand of Fate

Mirror, Mirror . . .

The Burning Pendulum

Ghost of Shady Lane

To learn more about this series by Dotti
Enderle, visit http://teen.llewellyn.com.

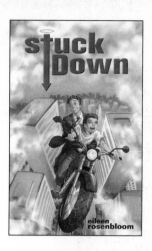

Stuck Down
by Eileen Rosenbloom

Can Kevin find his way back to heaven? After a yelling match with his dad, teenaged Kevin went skiing and suffered a fatal accident. Since his death seven months ago, he has quickly adjusted to the afterlife in Nirvanaland—spending time with his girlfriend Nicole in a heavenly world of singing flowers, talking pets, and endless games.

His idyllic lifestyle is shattered when he volunteers to deliver a letter to his girlfriend's mother on Earth. A motorcycle crash lands him in jail and puts him face-to-face with Morty, a menacing "dweller" who prefers to spend the afterlife wreaking havoc on humankind.

Stripped of his powers, Kevin cannot return to Nirvanaland until he takes care of "unfinished business"—repairing the fragile relationship with his father. Convincing his dad—who is also the prosecuting attorney in Kevin's trial—that he's come back from the dead won't be easy. And if they can't reconcile their differences . . . Kevin will be stuck on Earth forever.

ISBN 0-7387-0658-2

$8.95

WHERE WOULD YOU LIKE TO GO?

Got ideas?

Llewellyn would love to know what kinds of books you are looking for but just can't seem to find. Fantasy, witchy, occult, science fiction, or just plain scary—what do you want to read? What types of books speak specifically to you? If you have ideas, suggestions, or comments, write Megan at:

megana@llewellyn.com

Llewellyn Publications
Attn: Megan, Acquisitions
2143 Wooddale Drive
Woodbury, MN 55125-2989 USA
1-800-THE-MOON (1-800-843-6666)
www.llewellyn.com